Isla snatched up some fresh towels from her trolley, desperate to hide the slight bulge of her belly.

She was desperate to occupy her hands in case they were tempted to remove that imperious look off Rafe's too-handsome face. Or worse—pull his head down to crash his mouth against hers to make her forget everything but the heat and fire of his masterful, mesmerizing, bone-melting kiss.

"I work at this hotel. Now, if you'll let me finish your room, I'll get out of your way and—"

"I thought you were going back to London to resume your fine arts degree." A frown tugged at his brow, his green-and-brown-flecked gaze holding hers with the force of a searchlight. "Wasn't that the plan?"

"I—I changed my mind." Isla swung away and strode into the bathroom with the towels. She placed the new ones on the towel racks and then gathered up the damp ones, bundling them against her body like a barrier. Her plans had changed as soon as she found out she was pregnant.

Everything had changed.

Secret Heirs of Billionaires

There are some things money can't buy...

Living life at lightning pace, these magnates are no strangers to stakes at their highest. It seems they've got it all... That is, until they find out that there's an unplanned item to add to their list of accomplishments!

Achieved:

1. Successful business empire.

2. Beautiful women in their bed.

3. *An heir to bear their name?*

Though every billionaire needs to leave his legacy in safe hands, discovering a secret heir shakes up the carefully orchestrated plan in more ways than one!

Uncover their secrets in:

The Sicilian's Secret Son by Angela Bissell

Claimed for the Sheikh's Shock Son by Carol Marinelli

Shock Heir for the King by Clare Connelly

Demanding His Hidden Heir by Jackie Ashenden

The Maid's Spanish Secret by Dani Collins

Sheikh's Royal Baby Revelation by Annie West

Look out for more stories in the
Secret Heirs of Billionaires series coming soon!

Melanie Milburne

CINDERELLA'S
SCANDALOUS SECRET

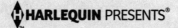

HARLEQUIN PRESENTS®

ISBN-13: 978-1-335-47866-5

Cinderella's Scandalous Secret

First North American publication 2019

Copyright © 2019 by Melanie Milburne

Printed in U.S.A.

Melanie Milburne read her first Harlequin novel at the age of seventeen, in between studying for her final exams. After completing a master's degree in education, she decided to write a novel, and thus her career as a romance author was born. Melanie is an ambassador for the Australian Childhood Foundation and a keen dog lover and trainer. She enjoys long walks in the Tasmanian bush. In 2015 Melanie won the HOLT Medallion, a prestigious award honoring outstanding literary talent.

Books by Melanie Milburne

Harlequin Presents

The Tycoon's Marriage Deal
A Virgin for a Vow
Blackmailed into the Marriage Bed
Tycoon's Forbidden Cinderella

Conveniently Wed!

Bound by a One-Night Vow
Penniless Virgin to Sicilian's Bride

One Night With Consequences

A Ring for the Greek's Baby

The Scandal Before the Wedding

Claimed for the Billionaire's Convenience
The Venetian One-Night Baby

Wedlocked!

Wedding Night with Her Enemy

Visit the Author Profile page
at Harlequin.com for more titles.

To Liza Fick,

I hope you enjoy this book dedicated specially to you.

Best wishes,

Melanie Milburne

CHAPTER ONE

THE PENTHOUSE IN the grand old Edinburgh hotel was the last room on Isla's shift. The irony didn't escape her that she was now cleaning penthouses rather than occupying them.

She knocked on the door and called out, 'House-keeping.' When there was no answer she swiped her pass key, opened the door and brought her cleaning trolley inside.

It was like stepping into another world—a world she had once briefly visited and fooled herself she could belong to... Had it only been five months ago?

Isla placed a protective hand over the slight swell of her abdomen, where the soft flutter of tiny developing limbs moving in their sac of amniotic fluid reminded her that in another four months her life would change yet again.

For ever.

Isla closed the door of the suite, tried too to close the door on her thoughts, but they lingered, floating around her head like black crows circling above a carcass. The carcass of her short but passionate relationship with her baby's father.

Rafe Angeliri, who didn't even know he was going to be a father.

'Relationship' was probably too generous a word to describe what she had experienced with Rafe. A fling. An affair. Two months of madness. Magical, mind-altering, body-fizzing madness. Two months where she had forgotten who she was, where she came from, what she represented. They had met in a bar and in under an hour she had ended up in bed with him. Her first ever one-night stand—except it hadn't been a one-night stand because Rafe had asked to see her again. And again. And again. And within a few days they were enmeshed in a passionate relationship she hadn't wanted to end.

But it had.

She had made it end.

Isla swept her gaze over the plush furnishings of the suite. During her fling with Rafe, spending a night in a luxury room such as this had become the norm. Sleeping between one thousand thread Egyptian cotton sheets, sipping French champagne from sparkling crystal flutes, eating at Michelin starred restaurants, wearing designer clothes and shoes and glittering jewellery that cost more than a car. Going to charity balls and opera and theatre shows and premiere red carpet events dressed like a supermodel instead of a foster kid from the wrong side of the tracks.

Trailer trash, tarted up to look like royalty.

The penthouse had been slept in the night before—the bed was rumpled on one side, the covers thrown back over the mattress in a way that snagged on her memory like a rose thorn on silk. Even the air smelled faintly familiar—a subtle blend of bergamot and citrus that made the skin on Isla's arms lift in a tide of goosebumps, the hairs on her scalp tightening, tingling, tensing at the roots. The room seemed to have a strange energy, as if the presence of a strong personality had recently disturbed the air particles and they hadn't quite yet recovered.

Isla gave herself a concussion-inducing mental slap, strode to the bed and stripped the linen off like a magician ripping a tablecloth from under a full setting of crockery. She had work to do and she couldn't allow her imagination to get the better of her. She had made her own metaphorical bed and she was happy to lie on it.

Alone.

Telling Rafe about her pregnancy had never been an option. How could it be? She couldn't risk him pressuring her into a termination. Couldn't risk him rejecting her *and* the baby. She had experienced repeated rejections throughout her childhood. Even her own father had sent her back to foster care for others to raise. How could she risk Rafe sending her away? She couldn't risk him offering to marry her out of a sense of duty. She knew first-hand how duty-motivated marriages worked out—with unwanted, unloved, unnurtured kids ending up in long-term foster care.

Isla remade the bed with the fresh linen from the trolley, stretching it over the mattress and straightening it to perfection, plumping up the pillows and neatly arranging them, along with the navy-blue scatter cushions and throw rug for the end of the bed. She stepped back to admire her handiwork when the door of the suite opened behind her.

Isla turned to face the guest with her best apologetic housemaid smile in place. 'I'm sorry. I'm not quite fin...'

Her smile faded along with her apology and her heart leapt like a ping-pong ball and lodged high and tight in her throat. She couldn't find her voice, couldn't stop her heart from thudding against her chest wall like it was trying to punch its way out. *Bumph. Bumph. Bumph.* Her skin tightened all over her body, pulling away from her skeleton in panic. She ran her eyes over her baby's father before she could stop herself, her gaze drawn to him by a force the passage of time hadn't changed. There should be a law against looking so good, so fit and healthy and virile. So very irresistible.

Unlike her, Rafe Angeliri hadn't changed in the three months since she had seen him last. His dark blue designer business suit and crisp white shirt paid homage to the superior athletic build it covered. Long muscled legs, broad chest and toned arms and an abdomen so hard and flat you could have cracked open a coconut. The open neck of his shirt revealed the tanned column of his throat and a tiny glimpse of masculine black chest hair. Aftershave-model-handsome, tall and lean with a clean-shaven, take-no-prisoners jaw, he commanded a room just by entering it. His slightly wavy black hair was neither long nor short but somewhere stylishly in between, brushed back from his intelligent forehead and curling against the edges of his shirt collar. The loosely casual hairstyle belied the relentless drive and meticulous focus of his personality.

However, his hazel eyes were even more cynical and there were vertical lines running down each side of his mouth that hadn't been there before.

But there was one other difference Isla detected before he quickly masked it—shock. It rippled across his features, sharpened his gaze, froze his movements until he was as still as a marble statue. But only for a microsecond. He had always had far better self-control than anyone she knew, certainly better than her, and yet she had always prided herself on her ability to mask her feelings. How else had she survived all those childhood foster home placements with perfect strangers?

'Isla.' Rafe gave a nod that somehow managed to be both formal and insulting. 'To what do I owe the pleasure of finding you waiting beside my bed?'

Isla stepped away from the bed as if it had suddenly burst into flames. Being anywhere near a bed when Rafe was within touching distance was a bad idea. A very tempting but bad, bad, *bad* idea. They had spent more time in bed than out of it during their short and volatile fling. Sex had brought them together in a thunderclap of attraction at their first meeting in a bar—an explosion of lust that had sent shockwaves through her entire body. She hadn't really enjoyed sex until she experienced it with Rafe. It had been out of this world sex and even now she could feel the memories of it coursing through her body. Little pulses and tingles in her flesh—the flesh he had awakened with his lips and tongue, as if being in the same room as him triggered her body into remembering, longing, *wanting*.

Isla snatched up some fresh towels from her trolley, desperate to hide the slight bulge of her belly. No one was going to be cracking coconuts on her abdomen any time soon. She had never had a particularly flat stomach, which made her hope Rafe wouldn't notice the slight change in it now. It had always surprised her that he had found her so attractive. She was nothing like the super-slim and glamorous women he normally dated. She was desperate to occupy her hands in case they were tempted to slap that imperious look off his too-handsome face. Or worse—pull his head down to crash his mouth against hers to make her forget everything but the heat and fire of his masterful, mesmerising, bone-melting kiss.

'I work at this hotel. Now, if you'll let me finish your room, I'll get out of your way and—'

'I thought you were going back to London to resume your Fine Arts degree?' A frown tugged at his brow, his green and brown flecked gaze holding hers with the force of a searchlight. 'Wasn't that the plan?'

'I...I changed my mind.' Isla swung away and strode into the bathroom with the towels. She placed the new ones on the towel racks and then gathered up the damp ones, bundling them against her body like a barrier. Her plans had changed as soon as she found out she was pregnant.

Everything had changed.

Rafe followed her into the palatial bathroom, his presence shrinking it to the size of a tissue box. Isla caught a glimpse of herself in the mirror over the twin basins and inwardly groaned. She had never been more conscious of her lack of make-up, the dark circles under her eyes, the lankness of her red-gold hair under her housemaid's cap. Or the secret swell of her belly beneath her housemaid's white frilly apron. Was he comparing her to his latest lover? She had seen photos of him with numerous women in the time since she had brought their relationship to an end. She wondered if it had been deliberate on his part—to be seen out and about with as many women as possible as an *I'll show you how quickly I can move on from you* slap to her ego. After all, Isla had been the one to end their fling, which clearly wasn't something he was used to. Women were queuing up to be with him, not rushing to leave.

'That was rather sudden, was it not?' His voice contained a note of scepticism that matched the piercing focus of his gaze. 'I thought you liked living in London?'

Isla sucked in her tummy to her backbone. She straightened the toiletries on the marble counter for something to do with her hands, annoyed they weren't as steady as she would have liked. 'I felt ready for a change of scene. Anyway, I could no longer afford living in London.'

His top lip curled and his glittering eyes pulsated with barely controlled anger. 'Is there someone else? Is that why you called time on us?'

Isla met his gaze in the mirror, her stomach free-falling at the bitterness shining in his eyes. 'Us? We weren't an "us" and you know it. It was a fling, that's all, and I wanted it to end.'

'Liar.' The word came out like a bullet. Hard. Direct. Bullseye. 'At least have the decency to be honest with me.'

Honest? How could she be honest about anything about herself? About her background. About her shame. It didn't matter if she was wearing haute couture or hand-me-downs, the shame burned like a flame inside her. 'There's no one else. I told you in my note—I simply wanted out.'

Finding out she was carrying Rafe's baby had thrown Isla into a terrifying world of uncertainty. The thought of him rejecting her, throwing her and their baby out of his life like her father had done to her had been too painful. She couldn't think of any way she could tell him about her pregnancy that wouldn't cause irreversible destruction in his life. She hadn't known him long enough or well enough to trust he wouldn't try and pressure her into having an abortion. Not that she would have allowed him or anyone to do that. She had enough doubts about her own mothering ability. She had been in and out of foster care since she was seven; her memories of her own mother were patchy at best, painful at worst. What sort of mother would *she* make? It was a constant nagging toothache type of worry that kept her awake at night. The doubts and fears throbbed on the inside of her skull like miniature hammers.

'Ah, yes. Your note.' There was a disparaging bite to Rafe's tone.

Isla forced herself to hold his searing gaze. She put on her game face, the one she had perfected over the years. The face that had helped her survive yet another placement with strangers. The mask of cool indifference that belied the churning, burning, yearning emotions fighting for room in her chest.

'You're the one who needs to be honest. You're

only angry because I was the one to leave you. But you would've called time sooner rather than later. None of your flings last longer than a month at the most. I was already on borrowed time.'

A muscle worked in the lower quadrant of his jaw, his eyes still brewing and boiling with bitterness. 'Couldn't you have waited until I got home from New York to speak to me face to face? Or is that why you didn't come with me on that trip while I negotiated that deal? Because you'd always planned to leave while I was away. You didn't want to risk having me try to change your mind.'

Isla pressed her lips together, struggling to keep her own temper in check. She had known how important that deal was to him. The biggest of his career. The man he was negotiating the deal with was a deeply religious family man who might not have signed off on the deal if news broke about Rafe's pregnant lover with the salacious background. She had started to feel nauseous just before he'd suggested she come with him to New York. Thinking at first it was a mild stomach bug, she had decided to stay at his villa in Sicily while he went abroad. She had gone everywhere else with him during their two months together, slotting into his life without giving too much thought as to why she shouldn't be subsuming her life so readily, so recklessly into his. But then a wriggling worm of suspicion about the possibility of pregnancy had tunnelled into her brain to such a degree it was all she *could* think about. She'd had to know one way or the other. And she'd wanted to be alone when she did. She hadn't wanted him finding her with a test wand in her hand, or finding her bent over the toilet heaving her insides out.

Once she'd seen the test was positive, she'd known what she had to do.

End it.

End their fling and get the hell out of his life before more harm was done. Because she would have brought him harm. Great harm. Harm from which there would be no easy recovery. The Pandora's Box of her past would have created havoc and mayhem in his well-to-do circles. The New York deal would have been compromised—the deal he had worked on for months and months. One leaked photo of her in lingerie, dancing in that sleazy gentlemen's supper club, and Rafe's desire to chair a prominent children's charity would be destroyed. Future business deals of his would be jeopardised from the stain of her background.

Isla had pictured the headlines—*Exotic dancer pregnant with billionaire Italian hotelier Raffaele Angeliri's love-child!* He would not have come back from that easily, if at all. Scandals stuck to high-profile people, sometimes for the rest of their lives. She couldn't do it to him; she couldn't do it to their child. To have it surrounded by shame from the moment it was born, even *before* it was born.

Isla raised her chin and chilled her gaze to freezing. 'You wouldn't have been able to change my mind.'

His eyes went to her mouth and then back to her gaze. 'Are you sure about that, *cara*?' His voice was a deep gravelly burr that was as wickedly sensual as a slow stroke of one of his hands between her legs. And his smouldering gaze threatened to scorch her eyes out of her head and leave two smoking black holes in their place.

Isla swung away from the marble counter, grabbing the used towels from the rack. She had to get away from him before she did or said something she would regret. Like, *Guess what I'm hiding underneath this apron? Your baby.* Of course, a part of her—a huge part—believed he had a right to know he was to become a father. And if she had come from a similar background to his she would have told him upfront—no question about it.

But they came from different worlds and there was no way she could see to bridge the deep chasm that divided her world from his.

'Leave that.' He gestured with his hand at the towels she was carrying, a frown etched between his eyes. 'Why are you cleaning hotel rooms? Surely you could have picked work more in line with your artistic aspirations?'

Isla kept the towels against her body. She needed whatever armour she could use against his disturbingly potent presence. Damp towels were hardly going to cut it, but still. 'I'm working for a friend, helping her out. She runs a cleaning agency—Leave It to Layla and Co. You might have heard of it?' She knew she was rambling, sounding as flustered as she felt. It annoyed her to be so on edge because she had always prided herself on her acting ability. Hadn't she spent most of her life pretending to be someone she wasn't?

Rafe's gaze was unwavering. 'I haven't but I'll keep the name in mind. I'm thinking about buying this hotel. That's why I'm staying here under an assumed name to see how things work behind the scenes.'

'Don't you have enough hotels by now?' Isla didn't hold back on the sarcasm in her tone. 'I mean, you nailed that New York deal, didn't you? One of your biggest, right?'

If he was proud of his achievements he didn't show it in his expression. She might as well have been commenting on how many shirts and ties he'd collected since their breakup. One side of his mouth lifted in a smile that wasn't quite a smile. 'Nice to know you've been taking a keen interest in my business affairs.'

Argh. Why had she made it sound as if she was poring over the newspapers for every little snippet of information about him? Isla affected a bored expression to make up for lost ground, moving past him to go back to the main part of the suite. 'Look, I really need to finish this suite. My shift ends in a few minutes.'

He caught one of her arms on her way past, his fingers a deceptively gentle bracelet around the fine bones of her wrist. Her skin reacted to his touch, every nerve standing up to take notice—remembering, wanting, needing. 'Stay and have a drink with me.' His voice had dropped to that same low deep burr that made the base of her spine fizz like thousands of bubbles in top shelf champagne.

'No can do.' Isla pulled her wrist away, pointedly rubbing at her skin. 'I have another engagement.' The lie slipped so easily from her lips, but then she had a Master's degree in face-saving deceit.

Something moved at the back of his gaze as quick as a camera shutter click. Disappointment? Pain? Anger? She couldn't quite tell. 'I'm sure they won't mind waiting.'

Isla lifted her chin, locking her defiant gaze on his. She could feel the tug-of-war between their two strong wills prickling and pulsing in the air like soundwaves. The push and pull of their personalities had more or less defined their whirlwind fling. 'You can't force me to do anything any more, Rafe.'

His eyebrows lifted ever so slightly above his

hazel eyes. And his cynical half-smile was back. 'When did I ever force you, *cara mia*? You were with me all the way, *sì*?' His voice was so low and deep it sounded like it was coming through the floor-boards. Deep enough to strike a chord in the secret core of her being, reverberating like the sound of a struck tuning fork.

Isla tried to block the storm of erotic memories that flooded her brain. Memories of her limbs en-tangled with his, her body singing with delight and satiation and super-heightened sensuality. The taste of him, the musky scent of their coupling in the air, the feel of his hands lazily stroking the flank of her thigh, so close to the pounding heart of her need. She drew in a sharp breath and went back to her trolley, grasping the handle to stop herself from touching him. Surely she was immune to him by now? She hadn't felt a flicker of lust for anyone since they'd broken up.

She wondered if she ever would again.

'I have to go.' Isla pushed the trolley towards the door but before she could get any distance his voice stalled her.

'One drink. In the bar downstairs. I promise I won't keep you long.' A tiny pause and he added, 'Please, *cara*?'

Isla should have walked out without saying an-other word but something in the quality of his tone stopped her. If she refused it would make her look churlish. After all, she had been the one to end their relationship. If anyone should be feeling churlish it should be him. She had left a note at his home rather than tell him face to face. The most telling thing about their breakup was that she'd only received one phone call from him where he'd left a stinging voice-mail. One final call that had allowed him to vent his anger and thus confirming to her she had done the right thing. If he had truly cared about her, wouldn't he have called multiple times? Wouldn't he have done everything in his power to find her? To meet with her in person and beg her to come back to him. Except men like Rafe Angeliri didn't beg. They didn't have to. Women never left him in the first place. They were the ones who begged to stay.

But spending time with Rafe was dangerous for her now. Dangerous on so many levels. She was only just starting to show her pregnancy; her bump was still in that *is-she-or-isn't-she?* phase. A quick drink might be just enough contact to assure him she had well and truly moved on with her life. Moved on from *him*. Surely she owed him a few more minutes of her time? He was the father of her baby, even if she'd vowed never to let him know it. She would look upon having a quick drink with him as a fact-finding mission. She needed to know what his plans were so she could adjust her own. If he was going to spend time here in Edinburgh then she would have to leave. To disappear and hope he wouldn't come looking for her.

Isla turned to face Rafe, her heart and mind still at war. When had she ever been able to resist him? A big fat never. Which was why she had to be careful around him now. 'Okay. One drink.'

Once the door closed behind Isla, Rafe let out a breath he hadn't realised he'd been holding. Five months had passed and he still couldn't be in the same room as her without wanting her. The lust hit him like a sucker punch. Seeing her standing beside his bed had brought back so many memories. Memories he had never been able to erase from his mind, much less his body. It was as if Isla McBain had imprinted herself on his flesh. No one else could satisfy the burning, aching need she aroused. He had dated other women since but each time he had thought about sleeping with them something had made him pull back. He was turning into a damn monk and he had to sort it out so he could move on with his life.

Move on from *her*.

Rafe was annoyed at himself for still being bitter about their breakup. But usually it was him who called time on his relationships. He was the one who set the agenda and changed it when it suited him. It had been a new experience—an uncomfortable experience— to have Isla leave him, especially when he was out of town working on the biggest and most important deal of his career. And especially when he had taken her home to Sicily—the first lover he had ever taken to his private sanctuary.

His villa in Sicily was normally out of bounds for casual lovers. It blurred the boundaries to have lovers sleep over too many times, but for once he had relaxed his guard. He had taken Isla there for weeks on end, cancelled important work meetings just so he could spend time with her without the press documenting every moment. Something about their relationship had made him want to keep it out of the public eye. Not because he didn't like being with her but because he did. A lot. A lot more than he had enjoyed being with other lovers.

But somehow he had read her wrong and that bothered him. Big time. What niggled him the most was that he suspected she had waited until he was preoccupied with that deal so she could maximise the impact.

Coming home to an empty villa and a note from Isla propped up on the mantelpiece had blindsided him. And if there was one thing he detested more than anything else it was being blindsided. Hadn't his duplicitous father set the bar for blindsiding? With his father's two families operating simultaneously—two wives, two families, who each thought they were Tino Angeliri's entire world until Rafe had discovered the truth when he was thirteen. A phone call from one of his father's staff had changed everything. Revealed everything. When his father had been critically injured in a car crash while away on business, the staff member had felt compelled to inform Rafe and his mother of Tino's life-threatening injuries. But when he and his mother flew to Florence to be by Tino's bedside they discovered Tino already had visitors. Four of them. His other family. His wife and two sons. His father's first family. His father's *official* family. His father's other life. Rafe had stood by the hospital bed and recounted every one of his father's blatant lies. Years and years of bold-faced blatant lies.

Rafe was his father's dirty little secret. His illegitimate son.

Coming home to that damn *Dear John* letter from Isla had enraged Rafe so much he had torn it into confetti-like shreds. It had reminded him of walking into that Florence hospital when everything he believed about himself and his family was found to be false. A pack of lies. Secrets and lies. He hadn't realised he was capable of such anger until it hit him in sickening, gut-shredding waves. Why hadn't he seen it coming? Surely there must have been a sign. Or had Isla deliberately misled him, lulling him into a false sense of security just as his father had done for all those years? Pretending, lying, misleading— the three deadly sins of any relationship.

He had called Isla as soon as he'd read the note

and left a message. It wasn't a message he was particularly proud of, but he was not one to hand out second chances. She hadn't called him back and, in a way, he had been glad. Clean breaks were always to be advised. But nothing about their breakup felt clean to him. It felt rough around the edges, torn instead of neatly cut, ripped and raw instead of resolved.

Rafe paced the floor of the penthouse until he was sure he would wear his way through the carpet to the suite below. Something was off about her now. Her body language, her averted gaze, her caginess. Why had Isla had given up her Fine Arts degree and moved back to Scotland? She had been so passionate about her art and had said how much she enjoyed living in London. He had seen some of her drawings and he'd been amazed at her talent. What had made her turn her back on her dreams and work for a friend in a job that didn't maximise her creativity? Had something happened in the time since their breakup? Something that had poisoned her artistic aspirations. But what?

He turned and looked at the neatly made bed, picturing her in it with her slim limbs wrapped around his. He let out a filthy curse and swung away, his guts twisting and tangling in disgust. Disgust at himself for allowing her to *still* get under his skin.

Isla was by far the feistiest and most fascinating woman he had ever been involved with and he couldn't help wondering if that was why no one else since had measured up. He had found Isla's quick wit and hair-trigger temper entertaining as well as frustrating. So few people stood up to him. So few women treated him as an equal instead of a meal ticket.

Isla had been different. She had made it virtually impossible for him to be satisfied by anyone else. He had enjoyed their heated debates, enjoyed how all their fights were settled between the sheets. He'd enjoyed goading her to get a rise out of her just so he could have her quaking and shuddering in his arms.

She looked the same but different somehow. Her figure was still slim but some of her curves had ripened, making him ache to touch her, to feel her, to smell and taste her. Her breasts were a little fuller. *Dio.* He had to stop thinking about her gorgeous breasts. How soft they felt in his hands, under his lips and tongue. How it felt to have her moving, thrashing beneath him as he took her screaming all the way to paradise.

The new energy that surrounded her now intrigued him. Her gaze blazing with defiance one minute and skittering away from his the next. Her skin paling and then flushing, her body turned away when before it had always turned towards him like a compass point finding true north.

Isla's rejection was like a scabbed-over sore. Seeing her again had ripped off the scab and left the wound smarting, stinging, festering. He had to expunge her from his system so he could finally move forward. One drink with her and he would walk away without a backward glance. He owed it to himself to leave what they'd shared in the past where it belonged.

It was over and the sooner he accepted it the better.

CHAPTER TWO

ISLA CHANGED OUT of her work uniform and back into her street clothes. Gone were the designer threads Rafe had bought her. She had left everything behind, wanting no reminders of their fling— other than the one she carried within her body. These days she wore practical and cheap off-the-peg casual outfits.

She stepped into her black leggings and pulled on her long-sleeved jersey top, but rather than disguise her shape, her clothes drew attention to it. She stroked her hand over the bulge of her belly. Surely the baby hadn't grown in the last few minutes? She pulled the garment away from her abdomen but as soon as she let it go it lovingly draped across her body as if to say, *Look at my baby bump!*

Isla picked up her jacket even though it was a little warm to wear it inside. She fed her arms through the sleeves and tied the waist ties around her middle. She glanced at herself again in the changing room mirror, doing her best to ignore the niggling of her conscience over the lengths she was going to in order to keep her pregnancy concealed from Rafe.

She took out her small make-up kit from her tote bag and did what she could to freshen up her features. Concealer—her new best friend—was first, followed by a tinted moisturiser and some strategically placed eyeshadow to bring out the blue in her eyes. She followed that up with bronzer, highlighter, lip-gloss and a decent coat of mascara, a part of her wondering why she was going to so much trouble. But, in a way, make-up was another form of armour and, God knew, she needed a heck of a lot of armour around Rafe Angeliri.

Isla released the ties of her jacket and skimmed her hand over her belly again. Was it her imagination or was her baby more active than usual? She was so used to calling it her baby but it was Rafe's baby too. The prod from her conscience was like the stab of a dart to the heart. *Rafe's baby.* Of course, he had a right to know. Hadn't she always believed that to be the case? His New York deal was finalised now, so why shouldn't she tell him about the baby? There was a risk he might reject the child, but she wouldn't insist on his involvement if he didn't wish it.

The thought of her baby being rejected by Rafe made her heart tighten. The last thing she wanted for her child was a reluctant father. Isla had experienced one of those and look how *that* had turned out. Rejection. It might as well have been her middle name instead of Rebecca. Years and years in and out of foster homes, never belonging to anyone, never being chosen for an open adoption. Never feeling loved.

No. Her baby deserved better and she would do everything in her power to give her child the best upbringing she could, with or without Rafe's support.

Isla drew in a shuddering breath and retied her jacket around her waist. She would look for an opportunity to tell him during their catch-up drink rather than dump it on him straight away. She knew that much about him—he didn't like surprises.

The hotel bar was downstairs on a mezzanine level and Isla walked in with a tight band of tension around her head and her stomach like a nest of agitated ants. Rafe was seated in a quiet corner on one of two burgundy-coloured leather chesterfield tub chairs and, as if he sensed the precise moment she arrived, he looked up from his phone and locked gazes with her. A zap of awareness shot through her body. They might as well have been the only people in the bar—the only people on the planet. The only people in the universe. She couldn't look away if she tried. Her gaze was tethered by his, her body under his command as if he had programmed her to his particular coordinates.

He was still wearing the dark blue business suit and white shirt but he had since put on a silver and black striped tie. That small gesture had a strange effect on her, momentarily ambushing her feelings.

Feminist she might be, but she had always admired his attention to the old-fashioned manners of dating. During their fling, she hadn't opened a single car door for herself. He had always walked on the road side of the footpath…he had never sat down before she was seated. It was so starkly different from the way other men in her past life had treated her and she had lapped it up, enjoying every moment of feeling like someone of value.

Rafe rose from the chair as she approached, his gaze sweeping over her in an assessing manner. 'You look very beautiful but I quite liked you in that sexy housemaid outfit.' His voice had a rough edge and his rich Italian accent seemed even more pronounced.

Isla had always been a sucker for his accent. She had worked on her regional Scottish accent for years, doing all she could to rid herself of any trace of her chaotic and underprivileged childhood. These days, no one would ever guess she hadn't been educated at an exclusive fee-paying Edinburgh school and that was the way she wanted it.

Isla gave him a stiff-lipped, no-teeth smile and, finally tearing her gaze away, sat in the chair beside his, placing her tote bag on the floor next to her chair. 'I hope there isn't a policy about hotel cleaning staff fraternising with guests but here goes.'

'If there is any issue I will deal with it,' Rafe said and then frowned. 'Don't you want to take off your coat? It's warm in here.'

'No. Not yet.' Isla couldn't meet his gaze and picked up the cocktails menu and pretended an avid interest in the selection.

'What would you like to drink?' Rafe signalled the drinks waiter.

'Something soft—lemonade.'

His ink-black eyebrows rose. 'What about some champagne? Or a cocktail? You used to love—'

'You know that saying: when life hands you lemons?' Isla sent him a wry look and leaned forward to place the cocktail menu back on the table between them. 'Suffice it to say, I've developed quite a taste for lemonade.'

Rafe gave the order for drinks to the waiter, who had just then approached, and once the young man had left Rafe turned back to study Isla's expression for a long moment. 'You don't seem yourself. Does my company distress you that much?'

Isla could feel the heat crawling into her cheeks and right now the last thing she needed was more warmth on her person. Her jacket was making her feel as if she were sitting in a sauna. 'It was quite a shock running into you like that while I was doing your room. I…I haven't quite recovered.' She was pleased with her response. It sounded reasonable and it was more or less the truth. She would probably *never* recover.

'Yes, indeed it was.'

The silence contained an undertow of tension that tugged at Isla's already fraught nerves.

The waiter came over with their drinks, setting them down in front of them and discreetly melting away.

Rafe watched Isla take a generous sip of her lemonade with a slight frown between his eyes as if he couldn't quite understand why she wasn't sipping a Bellini instead. The lemonade was cold and sweet but it did nothing to reduce the tide of colour she could feel in her cheeks. Beads of perspiration formed under her hairline and between her shoulder blades but the thought of removing her jacket and letting her body deliver the message for her was suddenly too daunting.

Isla put her glass back on the table and forced herself to meet his gaze. 'Why are you looking at me like that?'

'You're not happy.' It was a statement, not a question.

Isla pushed a strand of sticky hair back off her face, uncomfortable with his probing scrutiny. Uncomfortable that he could see things she had fought so hard to conceal. 'I hardly see why that is any business of yours.'

'I could have made you happy, *cara*.' The pitch of his voice lowered to a low growl of bitterness.

She crossed one leg over the other and moved her top foot up and down in jerky movements. 'How? By dressing me up like some sort of doll? A toy you played with only when the fancy took you. No thanks.'

A brooding frown entered his gaze. 'I told you how important that deal was to me. Bruno Romano was a nightmare to negotiate a coffee date with, let alone a hotel chain that size. I'm sorry if you read that as neglect.'

Isla picked up her glass of lemonade again, the ice cubes rattling against the glass betraying her nervousness in Rafe's presence. She had to find a way to tell him about the baby, but how? Meeting him like this was crazy, but hadn't she always been a little crazy where he was concerned? Her feelings for him were so confusing. There were times when she didn't even like him and yet her body adored him. Her body craved him like a powerful drug. Damn it, her body even *recognised* him. She could feel the tingles and fizzes moving through her flesh just by sitting within reach of him, every cell of her body vibrating.

She took another sip of her lemonade. 'So, why are you interested in this hotel? I didn't realise Scotland was on your radar.'

'It wasn't until I met you. You awakened my interest.' Rafe lifted his small dram of whisky to his mouth and took a measured sip, savouring the taste for a moment before he swallowed. Isla couldn't tear her gaze away from the up and down movement of his tanned throat, her eyes drifting to the dark stubble around his mouth and jaw. She tightened her hand around her glass, remembering how it felt to run her fingertips over that sexy regrowth, remembering the way it felt grazing against the soft skin of her breasts. On her inner thighs…

She glanced at him again with her making-polite-conversation expression in place. 'So, are you going to buy it?'

He cradled the whisky glass in two hands, his long strong fingers overlapping. That was another thing she remembered—how those clever fingers could wreak such havoc on her senses when they got down to business on her body. His gaze tethered hers in a lock that made her inner core contract like the tightening of a small fist. 'I like what I've seen so far.' Somehow, she didn't think he was still talking about the hotel.

Isla released a shuddery breath and took another sip of her lemonade, acutely conscious of his probing gaze. She was too warm from still wearing her jacket, or maybe it was being within touching distance of the man who had scorched every inch of her body with his touch.

Rafe leaned forward and put his whisky glass on the small table between their chairs and then sat back, his hands resting on his thighs. 'Tell me why you quit your Fine Arts degree.'

Isla shrugged one shoulder and rolled one of her ankles to burn off restless energy. *You should have told him by now.* Her conscience was jabbing at her but she couldn't work up the courage. 'I lost interest after I came back to the UK. I'd already missed half of one semester by staying in Italy with you. I only planned on going for a two-week sketching holiday if you remember.'

'But you could have made it up, surely?'

'I couldn't be bothered.' She looked into the contents of her glass rather than hold his gaze. 'It was a pipe dream to think I could make a career out of painting portraits. I decided it wasn't worth the effort of trying.'

His frown deepened. 'But surely cleaning hotel rooms isn't going to satisfy you long-term?'

Pride stiffened Isla's shoulders and sharpened her gaze. 'Careful, Rafe. Your privileged upbringing is showing. Anyway, my friend Layla has made a career out of it—or is starting to.'

'But you're an artist, not a businesswoman.'

Isla affected a laugh. 'You make it sound like you know me. You don't.'

'I know you well enough to know you will not be satisfied unless you express your creativity.' Rafe leaned forward so his forearms were resting on his thighs, his gaze trained intently on hers. 'I have a proposition for you. Business, not personal.'

Isla raised her brows. 'Oh? Let me guess... You want me to paint your portrait?'

He gave a twisted smile. 'No. My grandmother, actually. My mother's mother. She's about to turn ninety. She's difficult to please. I don't think she's liked a single thing I've bought for her. But I thought a portrait would make a nice birthday present for her.'

Isla chewed at one side of her mouth. How ironic her first ever commission offer came from Rafe. Of course, she couldn't accept. But the thought of the money he might be prepared to pay her gave her pause. Why would he want to commission *her*, though? Did he think he could talk her into another fling with him? But, even so, she couldn't help feeling intrigued about his family. He had rarely mentioned anything about his background and she'd been deliberately evasive about hers. They had somehow come to a tacit agreement to leave the topic of families alone.

'Surely there are other artists, much more established artists, you could commission?' she asked.

'I want you.' His eyes glittered with something that seemed to suggest it wasn't just her artistic ability he was solely interested in.

The thought of resuming their affair was strangely exciting. Thrilling and exciting and dangerous.

But completely and utterly out of the question.

Isla leaned forward to put her drink on the table and began to rise from her chair. 'I'm sorry. I'm not available.'

Rafe placed a hand on her knee before she could stand, locking his gaze with hers. 'Think about it, Isla. You can name your price.'

She was close enough to him to smell his citrus-based aftershave. Close enough to see the flecks of brown and green in his eyes that made his irises look kaleidoscopic. The warm press of his hand on her knee sent a wave of heat straight to her core, stirring wickedly erotic memories in her flesh.

The air seemed to vibrate with energy. Sexual energy so powerful she could feel its *tug-tug-tug* on her insides, reminding her of the wickedly erotic delights she had experienced in his arms. Delights she had not been able to erase from her memory. They were seared into her brain and body so that every time he was within reach of her, her flesh tingled and prickled with excitement.

Isla knew she had to put a stop to this. Right here. Right now. She couldn't agree to spending time with Rafe—not under any circumstances. He'd said she could name her price but wouldn't *she* be paying the biggest price in the end? She pushed his hand off her knee. 'Rafe, there's something I need to tell you…'

'What?'

She brought her gaze to his and swallowed against the restriction in her throat. 'The reason I left you so abruptly…' *Oh, God, why was this so difficult?* 'I was scared about how you'd react and I—'

A frown carved into his forehead. 'Did you cheat on me? Tell me, Isla. Were you unfaithful?' His tone contained more hurt than anger. It seemed to bruise the atmosphere like mottled clouds.

Isla had a strange desire to laugh at the absurdity of the notion of her being unfaithful. He was the most amazing, exciting, thrilling lover and she had missed him every day since. And probably would for the rest of her life. No one would ever rise above the benchmark he had set. 'No, of course not. No, it wasn't anything like that.'

'Then what was it?'

She took a deep breath and slowly released it. 'I'm…pregnant.'

He looked at her blankly as if he hadn't registered what she'd said.

'Rafe, I'm having a baby.' She undid the ties from around her waist, gradually revealing the swell of her abdomen. His eyebrows drew together as realisation slowly dawned on his features, leaching him of colour, stiffening every muscle on his face.

'You're…*pregnant*?' His voice sounded nothing like his. Locked. Tight. Strangled. His Adam's apple bobbing up and down, a host of emotions flickering over his face—shock, horror, anger. And, yes, hurt. Waves of it rippling like an eddying tide.

Isla pressed her hands together in her lap. *Here it comes. The rejection.* Cold dripped into her stomach, the icy shards slicing at her insides. *I'm so sorry, little baby. This is all my fault.* 'I didn't want to tell you because—'

He opened and closed his mouth a couple of times

as if his voice had momentarily deserted him. 'Is it…mine?'

'I…' Her voice deserted her for a moment as the pain of his question hit home. Of course, he had every right to ask but it hurt to think he thought her capable of such betrayal. She might not have been honest with him about her background but she would never cheat on a partner. It went against her moral code.

His eyes drilled into hers. 'Answer the question, damn it.'

Isla gave a single nod. 'Yes. Of course, it is. I'm sorry I didn't tell you before—'

Rafe shot to his feet like his chair had exploded. 'Wait—I'm not having this discussion in a freaking wine bar. Upstairs. Now.' His voice had that commanding edge that never failed to put her back up like a cornered cat.

'I don't think that's a good idea right now—'

'You will do as I say. You owe me that, surely?' His mouth was pulled so tight his lips were almost bloodless, his eyes flashing with livid sparks of anger.

Isla put up her chin. 'You can tell me to get out of your life here. You don't need me to go up to your room.'

He flinched as if she had struck him. 'Is that how poorly you think of me?'

Isla no longer knew what to think. He wasn't acting the way she'd expected. He was angry, yes, but for some reason she sensed he was angrier with himself than with her. She didn't want to create a scene in a public place so gave in with as little grace as possible, not wanting him to think he could boss her around like one of his employees. She rose from her chair like a sulky teenager being sent to her room, her mouth set in a stubborn line. She hoisted her tote bag strap onto her shoulder and sent him a mutinous glare. 'You can cool it with the caveman routine. You should know by now it doesn't work with me.'

'Nothing seems to work with you, does it?' Rafe's tone was so cutting it shredded her already frayed nerves like a sword slashing satin ribbons. He led her to the private elevator that went to his penthouse, his fingers firmly cupping her elbow. He stabbed at the call button, his expression thunderous, but underneath that dark brooding tension Isla could see tiny flickers of hurt. And it shamed her. She hadn't thought in any detail about how he would feel if he ever found out about the pregnancy. Or at least she had tried *not* to think about it. She had been too concerned about protecting him from her past, protecting herself from the shame of it being splashed over every newspaper or online news or gossip outlet. She had fooled herself into thinking Rafe would be better off not knowing about his love-child—that it was easier for her to disappear than to risk him demanding she marry him or insist she have an abortion.

The elevator trip to the penthouse was conducted

in a silence so thick Isla could feel it pressing against her like a dense invisible fog. Every breath she took in caught at the back of her throat, every second that passed heightened the tension in her body until she thought she would snap. The mirrored walls reflected Rafe's demeanour—the tension rippling across his features as if he was recalling every moment of their fling and wondering how it had come to this point.

'Rafe, I—' she began.

'Wait until we are inside.' His tone was as commanding as a drill sergeant and the elevator doors whooshed open as if they too were frightened to disobey his orders.

Isla followed him into the penthouse, the door closing behind him with a resounding *kerplunk* that set her stomach churning fast enough to make butter. She let her bag drop to the floor with a thump, her legs feeling so feeble that they might go from beneath her. Tension was building behind her eyes and she worried she might be getting another one of the debilitating headaches that had plagued her during early pregnancy.

He came to where she was standing, his gaze focused, direct, searching. 'So, let me get this straight. You knew you were pregnant *before* you left?'

Isla drew in a shaky breath. 'Yes…'

His own inward breath sounded sharp and painful and he swallowed a couple of times, the tanned column of his throat moving up and down in an almost convulsive manner. 'How did it happen?'

'The usual way...'

He made an impatient sound in his throat. 'You told me you were on the Pill and I always used condoms. You can't get much safer than that.' His gaze sharpened with accusation. 'Unless you *lied* to me?'

'I was on the Pill but I might have compromised its effectiveness that weekend we went to Paris. I got a stomach bug, if you remember? And you didn't always use a condom.' She lifted her chin and forced herself to hold his gaze. 'We made love in the shower a couple of times without.'

Something passed through his gaze, as if he was recalling those passionate lovemaking sessions in intimate detail like replaying an erotic film. Images of them locked together with steamy shower water cascading over their rocking bodies. Images of him with his mouth sucking on her breast or her sucking on him, drawing his essence from him until he groaned out loud, his legs buckling at the knees. Or her with her hands flat against the marble walls of the shower with him driving into her from behind, her cries of earth-shattering pleasure filling the air. The warm cascading water. The slick press of their bodies. The need. The need. The need. The explosion of release that left them both gasping under the spray of the shower...

'And do you have a good reason for not telling me

you were pregnant before now?' His voice sounded as intimidating as a headmaster admonishing a recalcitrant student, but his eyes still pulsed with waves of hurt.

Isla hugged her arms around her middle, trying to keep control of her escalating emotions. 'I was worried you might pressure me into having a termination and—'

His frown was so deep it closed the space between his eyes. 'Do you really think I would do something like that? For God's sake, Isla. Surely you know me better than that?' His ragged tone contained deep notes of anguish along with the chord of anger.

Guilt rained down on her like hail, making her huddle further into herself, her gaze lowered from his. Had she made a mistake? Had she seriously misjudged him? Would it have been better to be honest with him from the outset? Hindsight was all very well, but she had thought she was doing the right thing at the time. The shock of finding out she was pregnant had thrown her completely. In her panicked state, it had felt safer to leave than have him send her away.

Hadn't she been sent away too many times in her childhood to count?

'I didn't know what to think,' Isla said, slowly raising her gaze back to his. 'I wasn't prepared to hang around long enough to risk you doing something radical like asking me to marry you or—'

'Well, at least you do know that much about me, because that's exactly what I plan to do.' The stridency in his voice was matched by the glint of determination in his gaze. 'I'm not having any child of mine grow up illegitimate. I want it to have my name and my protection. I can't—won't—accept any other alternative. We will be married as soon as it can be arranged.'

Isla's mouth dropped open and her stomach turned over. 'You can't be serious? We're practically strangers who—'

'We spent two months living and sleeping together. That's hardly what I'd call the action of strangers. We've made a child together. That's not something that I can approach in a casual manner. Formalising our relationship is the next step. The only step.' He walked over to the minibar and took out a bottle of mineral water, holding it up. 'Drink?'

Isla nodded; her mouth was so dry it felt like she had been licking the plush carpet at her feet. 'I can't marry you, Rafe. I *won't* marry you.'

'You can and you will.' His mouth had a stubborn set to it, his eyes now as hard as lichen-covered stones. 'I am not taking no for an answer.' He unscrewed the top of the mineral water with a loud hiss of released effervescence and poured it into two glasses and then turned back to hand her one.

Isla took the glass from him with a hand that was

visibly trembling. 'Rafe…be sensible about this. Marriage between us would never work.'

Lingerie waitress weds Sicilian hotel billionaire? How would she cope with the shame of her past splashed over every paper and news outlet?

'We will make it work for the sake of our child.' His jaw was set in an intractable line. 'How far along are you? Are you feeling well?' His tone softened a fraction, his eyes losing their hard glitter to be replaced by a shadow of concern. 'I'm sorry, I should have asked earlier.'

Isla put her glass down on a nearby table and then placed a hand on her small baby bump. 'I am now… I was more or less constantly sick for a couple of months. I'm five months into the pregnancy. I'm due around Christmas.'

His eyes went to where her hand was resting, his throat moving up and down over another swallow. He stepped closer, coming to stand in front of her. 'Can you feel the baby moving?'

'I started feeling it moving around the sixteen-week mark. Here—' She reached for his hand and laid it on the swell of her abdomen, watching his face as their baby gave tiny kicks. 'Can you feel it kicking? There—feel that?'

Rafe was standing so close she could see the dark and generous spray of stubble around his mouth and jaw. She could smell the sharp notes of citrus in his aftershave, redolent of sun-warmed lemons. She could feel the magnetic pull of his body making her ache to close the small distance to mesh her body to his—thigh to thigh, pelvis to pelvis. Why couldn't she be immune to him? Why did her body have to betray her? Could he sense the storm of hungry need he caused in her flesh? A need he had awakened.

His gaze softened in wonder as the baby moved against the press of his hand. 'That's amazing...' His voice became husky. 'Do you know the sex?'

'No. I didn't want to find out until the birth.'

The baby quietened and Rafe removed his hand and stepped back, his expression hardening once more. 'Were you *ever* going to tell me?' The note of accusation in his voice was sobering.

Isla moved to a little distance away so he wouldn't see how much she ached for him to hold her, to comfort her, to reassure her. *I was only trying to protect you.* The words were assembled like soldiers on the back of her tongue but she couldn't give the command for them to march forward. What good would it do? The less he knew about her reasons for not telling him the better. 'I decided it was better for both of us if I just quietly disappeared from your life.'

'*You* decided.' He spat the words out like bullets. 'You had no right to decide for *me*.' He thumped his fist against his chest for emphasis. 'I had a right to know I was to become a father. And my child has a right to know me. To have me in its life.' He swung away with a muttered curse, his hand scraping through the thickness of his hair so roughly she was surprised some of it didn't come out at the roots. He turned back and glared at her. 'For God's sake, Isla. Do you know how it feels for me to find out like this?'

Isla bit her lip, the tension in her head now feeling like needles poking into the back of her eyeballs. 'Look, I know it must be upsetting but—'

'Upsetting?' He gave a rough humourless laugh. 'Now that's an understatement. You denied me knowledge of my child. You planned to keep my child away from me indefinitely. Don't you think I have the right to be a little upset?'

Isla closed her eyes and pinched the bridge of her nose, trying to quell the stabbing pain behind her eyes. 'I was worried you would do exactly what you're doing. Barking commands at me as if I have no will of my own.' She dropped her hand from her face and sent him a defiant look. 'I will not marry you just because you insist on it. Lots of couples have babies together without marrying. And yes, even couples who are no longer together.'

His eyes clashed with hers in a battle she fought not to lose, but in the end, Isla was the first to look away. She couldn't cope with him when she was feeling so fragile. She couldn't cope with him, full stop. He was too commanding. Too directive. Too everything.

'You will marry me, Isla.' His voice had a steely

thread that sent a chill rolling down her spine like a runaway ice cube. 'For, believe me, you might not like the alternative. If there were to be a custody battle between us, I can assure you I will win it.'

The pain behind Isla's eyes intensified to a piercing drill that felt like it was burrowing deep into her brain. *Oh, God. Oh, God. Oh, God.* He was threatening to take her baby off her once it was born? He would be able to do it too. It wouldn't take too much digging into her background to cast doubt on her suitability as a mother. Those topless photos she'd stupidly been talked into doing for her 'portfolio', for instance. Who would ever believe she hadn't done them willingly? That she had been duped into making those shamelessly provocative poses, never realising how they might come back to haunt her. The photos alone might not be enough in a court of law to take her baby off her, but the thought of having those lewd photos out in public, splashed over newspapers and gossip magazines, was too much to bear.

Rafe's veiled threat only confirmed why she hadn't told him she was pregnant in the first place. He could be coldly ruthless when he needed to be. How else had he accumulated the amount of wealth he owned?

Her vision became blurred and the room began to tilt and sway as if gravity had been removed. She reached out her hand for the nearest solid object to stabilise herself but misjudged the distance. Her hand patted at mid-air and then a tide of nausea swept over her in an icy wave that prickled her scalp and sent pins and needles to her fingertips.

'Isla?'

She was vaguely conscious of Rafe's concerned tone but she couldn't get her voice to do anything much past a mumble. And then she folded like a rag-doll and slumped to the floor and everything faded to black...

Rafe rushed to Isla's slumped figure on the floor, his heart thumping in dread. 'Isla? Are you okay?' He was shocked at her pallid complexion—shocked and shamed that he had caused her to drop down in a faint.

He put her in the recovery position and then took her pulse, finding it more or less normal. A tornado of guilt assailed him, hammering into him with the force of knockout blows. He brushed the hair back from her clammy forehead, willing her to open her eyes. 'Come on, *cara*. Talk to me.'

What sort of man had he become in the last hour? It was unforgivable to harangue a pregnant woman into a state of collapse. Sweat broke out over his own forehead, remorse like bitter bile in his mouth. He was disgusted with himself, furious he had been so intent on communicating his ire that he hadn't considered her mental and physical state. She was pregnant, for God's sake—with *his* child.

He realised with a jolt of remorse that he hadn't even asked her how she felt about being pregnant. Whether or not the news had pleased her or shocked her. Had she considered other options? He would not have criticised her for considering a termination. He would not have criticised her for having one because he firmly believed it was a woman's choice what she did with her body. But there was a place deep inside his heart that felt relieved she hadn't chosen that path. *He was going to be a father.* It was still hard to get his head around but the evidence had kicked against his hand only minutes ago. 'Come on, *mio piccolo.* Talk to me.'

Isla slowly opened her eyes and groaned. 'My head aches…'

Rafe gently placed his palm on her forehead. 'I'll call an ambulance. I need to get you to hospital.' He reached for his phone in his trouser pocket but she placed a hand on his arm.

'No, please don't. It's just a tension headache. I've been getting them now and again. I don't need to go to hospital… I think it's because my blood sugar is a bit low.'

He helped her into a sitting position, cradling her around the shoulders with his arm, his other hand gently stroking the red-gold curls of her hair off her forehead. 'When did you last have something to eat?'

She gave a weary-sounding sigh. 'I don't know…

a few hours ago. I skipped lunch as I was running late and—'

'Right, well, that makes me all the more determined you're coming back with me to Italy,' Rafe said. 'You have to think about the baby. You can't go skipping meals and working long hours in a physically demanding job. Not when I can more than adequately provide for you.'

Isla gave him one of her combative looks but it didn't have its normal heat and fire. 'Must you be so bull-headed? I've told you I don't want to marry you.'

Rafe bit back a retort about her obeying his orders. He would raise the issue of marriage when she wasn't feeling so poorly. But he wasn't giving up. It wasn't in his nature to step back from a decision he'd made. He would never countenance walking away from his own flesh and blood. His own child. 'Let's leave the topic of marriage for later. For now, I'd like to see you with a bit more colour in your cheeks.' He brushed his fingers against the pale creaminess of her cheek. 'Do you think you can stand up? I'll help you to the bed so you can lie down for a bit. And I'll organise some food for you from Room Service.'

She looked like she was going to argue the point, but then sighed again and took hold of his proffered hand and he helped her into a standing position. She glanced up at him briefly, her teeth sinking into the fullness of her lower lip. 'I'm sorry for being such a nuisance…'

'Don't apologise,' Rafe said, leading her to the bed with his arm around her waist. 'I'm the one who should be apologising.'

Not just for upsetting her but for getting her pregnant. It took two to tango and how well they had tangoed. They had created a new life and it was up to him to make sure that new life was protected from now on. Protected and nurtured and provided for in every way a decent father could.

It still shocked him how slow he had been to realise Isla's condition. Why hadn't he noticed her slightly swollen tummy when he had first encountered her in his suite? Her uniform with its frilly apron had covered it reasonably well, so too the way she'd used towels and the trolley to hide her tell-tale shape. His only excuse for not noticing was that pregnancy had been the last thing on his mind when he'd found her in his room, standing next to his bed. He had been too intent on staring at her gorgeous mouth and breasts, recalling all the times he had sought pleasure from them.

Even now, with his arm around her waist, his body reacted to her closeness. Even the most casual touch produced a torrent of need within him. He had never experienced such fiery physical chemistry with anyone else. Her body fitted so perfectly against him as if they were two pieces of a complicated puzzle. He could smell the light flowery fragrance of her perfume and it evoked a host of memories—both good and bad. He had smelt that perfume for weeks in his villa after she'd left him. It had haunted him, tortured him.

Rafe helped Isla onto the bed and gently drew the cashmere throw rug over her curled up form. She looked so young and vulnerable and it sent another wave of guilt thrashing and crashing through him. Now was not the time for bitter recriminations and accusations. She clearly needed rest and better nutrition and it was up to him as her baby's father to provide it—regularly and consistently.

Her baby's father.

How strange to say those words. To have them applied to him. He had not thought of fatherhood in any detail before. It was something he'd thought he might look into one day in the future, but it certainly hadn't been on his to-do-soon list. His own father had not been the best role model, although in the early days his father had made Rafe feel special and loved. But then, at the age of thirteen, he'd found out that was nothing but a lie.

Rafe picked up the phone on the bedside table and ordered a nutritious meal and freshly squeezed fruit juice. Once the meal was ordered, he put the phone back in its cradle and sat on the edge of the bed next to Isla, taking one of her hands, and began stroking his thumb over the back of her hand. 'It shouldn't be too long. Do you want a mineral water or lemonade or something in the meantime?'

She opened her eyes and met his gaze. 'Why haven't you insisted on a paternity test?'

Rafe was ashamed to admit he had thought of doing exactly that, but something had stopped him. He wasn't one to hand out his trust too easily but, for some reason, he knew on a cellular level she was telling the truth. 'I figured I didn't need to confirm the baby is mine. You wouldn't have gone to so much trouble to avoid telling me if it was someone else's.'

Her gaze drifted to their joined hands, her teeth doing that lip-nibbling thing that always made him want to kiss her lip back into its soft, ripe shape. 'I won't stop you getting one if you want one.'

He gave her fingers a gentle squeeze. 'It won't be necessary.' He waited a beat before asking, 'When did you first suspect you were pregnant?'

'Just before you went to New York. I thought it was another stomach bug like in Paris, but then I realised I was a few days late...'

'It must have come as a shock.'

She glanced at him again, worry clouding her beautiful periwinkle-blue eyes. 'I was shocked and terrified. I didn't know what to do. Where to turn...'

If only she had turned to him. Why hadn't she? But he was reluctant to drill her with questions that might upset her in her current state. 'Did you consider...ending the pregnancy?'

She pulled her hand out of his as if his touch burned her. 'No. I'm sorry if you think I should've got rid of it but I couldn't. I have no problem with other women choosing that option but I didn't feel it was the right choice for me.'

Rafe took her hand again, holding it gently within his. 'I'm glad you didn't have a termination.' His voice came out rusty as he thought about the tiny life they had created. It felt surreal to be talking about a baby and yet it seemed the most natural thing in the world. Their baby. Created out of passion unlike any other he had experienced. It might not be love in the truest sense but surely it counted for something.

She looked at him with wide eyes. 'You are?'

Rafe stroked the back of her hand with his thumb. 'Like you, I believe it's a woman's choice what to do with her body but, while I can't deny I'm shocked at the news and still getting my head around becoming a father, I'm glad you chose to go ahead with the pregnancy. We will be good parents to our child, *cara.*'

A flicker of something passed through her gaze before it fell away from his. 'I'm sorry you found out the way you did.' Her forehead puckered in a frown. 'I should have told you at the beginning but I didn't feel I could take the risk.'

Rafe placed a finger over her lips to halt her speech. 'Hush now. You're supposed to be resting. What's done is done. It won't help either of us move forward if we keep rehashing the past. It's time to think of the future. The baby's future and ours.'

He lifted his finger from her petal-soft mouth, fighting to stop himself leaning down and covering her lips with his own. The fierce hunger he'd always felt for her was as stunning now as it had been in the beginning, when he had first locked gazes with her across a crowded bar. His blood heated to boiling, racing through his veins at rocket-force speed. He could feel the stirring of his groin—the hard swell of his flesh an erotic reminder of the heart-racing pleasure he had experienced so many times with her. Two months of phenomenal sex. Sizzling hot sex that he hadn't forgotten. He hadn't been able to erase it from his mind or his body. It had left echoes in his flesh he felt to this day. Being near her sent him into a frenzy of longing. It was all he could do to stop himself drawing her into his arms and reminding her of the red-hot passion they had shared.

But he had to ignore it. The baby was what mattered now. Rafe needed Isla to marry him so he could nurture and provide for their child. He just had to convince her to accept his proposal.

And convince her he would.

CHAPTER THREE

A SHORT TIME later Isla was propped up with pillows on Rafe's king-sized bed, the soft cashmere throw rug covering her legs, waiting for the meal he had ordered to arrive. The doorbell sounded in the suite and Rafe opened the door and the young male waiter—whom Isla had met once or twice in the staff quarters—brought in the Room Service silver service trolley. The waiter's brows rose when he saw Isla but, before she could explain why she was currently lying on a guest's bed, Rafe handed the young man a ridiculously generous tip and informed him that his fiancée would no longer be working for the hotel.

'But I haven't agreed to—' Isla began.

'Congratulations.' The young man beamed and pocketed the money. 'Thank you, sir. Much appreciated. I hope you enjoy your stay.'

'I'm already enjoying it immensely.' Rafe's tone contained a satirical note that set Isla's teeth on edge.

Once the waiter had gone, Isla glowered at Rafe

as he bent over her to place the tray of delicious food across her lap. *'Fiancée?* Did you listen to a word I said before about not marrying you?'

Once the tray was secure across her lap, Rafe sat on the edge of the bed beside her stretched out legs. 'I was only thinking of your reputation, *cara.* Do you want the staff of this hotel to gossip about the housemaid who leapt into bed with a guest? Becoming my fiancée offers you an element of respectability, does it not?'

He had made a good point but Isla didn't want to admit it. 'They'll gossip regardless. But that was your intention, wasn't it? Our supposed engagement will be all over the hotel and God knows how many social media platforms within minutes.'

'Good. It will save me making a formal announcement. Gossip works faster anyway.'

Isla ignored the food and kept glaring at him. 'I'm not going to be bullied into marrying you, Rafe. You might be used to getting your way in the business world but you won't get your way with me.'

One of his dark brows arched up and a glint appeared in his eyes. 'From memory, it only took me forty-two minutes to get you from the bar and into my bed the first day we met.'

Isla could feel the hot bloom of colour spreading across her cheeks. 'It won't happen again.'

He leaned closer to brush a lazy finger over the pool of pink in her cheek. 'Are you sure about that,

tesoro mio? Remember how good we were together.'
His low deep voice with its edge of huskiness was
doing serious damage to her resolve. 'So explosive,
sì?'

Isla suppressed a shiver. She remembered all too
well. She had never orgasmed with a partner before
Rafe. She had not enjoyed sex the way it was meant
to be enjoyed until his touch set her aflame. She wondered now if she would ever be able to make love
with anyone else. The thought of doing it with anyone else made her flesh crawl. 'Look, I know you
want to do the honourable thing and all that, but really, Rafe, marriage is going to ridiculous extremes.
We can still co-parent without—'

'I want my child to have my name and my protection,' Rafe said. 'I want him or her to live under
my roof so I can be involved in every aspect of its
upbringing. Part-time parenthood is not an option.'

Isla pushed the tray away to the other side of
the bed, her appetite completely deserting her. She
swung her legs over the side of the bed and stood. 'I
don't want to talk about it. Not now.' She moved over
to the windows to stand with her back to him, her
arms crossed over her chest. The sunshine had faded
and a bank of ominous-looking clouds had drifted in
from Arthur's Seat, making the dark fortress of Edinburgh Castle look all the more forbidding.

'Will you at least come back to Sicily with me?
Think of it as a holiday. Let me take care of you and

the baby and then you can make your final decision in a few weeks.' Rafe's voice had lost its commanding edge and it made it so much harder for her to think of a valid reason why she shouldn't go with him.

What did she have to lose by going with him? Just for a week or two until she began to feel a little stronger. Life had been a constant struggle since she'd left him. It had been hard trying to work and cope with gruelling nausea and the fatigue common in early pregnancy. If it hadn't been for her friend Layla helping her out with casual cleaning work at this hotel, Isla didn't know what she would have done. It wasn't as if she had a family network to call on to support her.

There was no one.

Or at least no one she *wanted* looking after her.

Isla turned to meet his gaze with her sceptical one. 'But will you accept my final decision?'

His expression gave no clue to what he was thinking or feeling. 'I will respect your decision once I am sure you're in the right frame of mind and healthy enough to make it.' He rose from the edge of the bed and picked up the tray and placed it on a nearby table. 'Now, eat this meal while I make the arrangements. We will leave tomorrow. Don't worry about packing—most of your things are still at my villa.'

Isla frowned. 'But…but why?'

'You didn't leave a return address. I decided to wait until I heard from you.'

'You weren't tempted to throw them all out?'

He gave her a wry smile. 'Oh, I was tempted. But I thought it would be much more satisfying to have you pick them up in person.'

Isla woke from a deep and refreshing nap to find herself alone in the penthouse. She got off the bed and stretched, feeling immensely relieved that all remnants of her headache had gone. For a moment she wondered if she should leave the hotel while she had the chance. Disappear before things got even more complicated. Remove herself from the temptation of Rafe's company. The temptation of his touch. But was running away again going to change anything? She was having his baby and he had a right to be involved in its upbringing. He had expressed a desire to be involved and she had to honour that.

But going to Sicily with him was a big step. A dangerous step, but the thought of continuing to work in a job she wasn't truly cut out for made her feel even more conflicted than spending a couple of weeks at Rafe's villa. Besides, she knew Layla had only given her the part-time work as a personal favour. She wouldn't be able to continue working much longer into the pregnancy anyway.

Isla fished her phone out of her tote bag and dialled Layla's number and briefly explained the situation.

'Seriously? You're going back to Sicily with him?'

Layla's voice rose in shock. 'But I thought you said you never wanted to see him again?'

Isla sighed. 'Yes, well, it seems I might have misjudged him a bit. He sounds really keen about the baby and is insisting on marrying me. Not that I've agreed to it or anything. How could I, given the difference in our backgrounds?'

'Marriage? Gosh, that's a bit extreme, isn't it?' Layla said.

'Those were exactly my words,' Isla said. 'He doesn't love me and the last thing I want to do is marry someone who doesn't love me. But I'm only going with him to Sicily for a short holiday. I figure I owe him that at the very least.'

'But your background might not be an issue for him. Have you thought of telling him about it? About the photos too?'

'I can't do either. I can't risk him looking at me like I'm something he wants to scrape off the bottom of his handmade Italian leather shoes.'

'Mmm, I hear you.' Layla sighed. 'But what if he doesn't? What if he doesn't care what happened in your past? You were with him two months without anyone finding out. Why would marrying him be any different?'

'We flew under the radar when it was just a fling,' Isla said. 'Can you imagine what press interest an announcement of our engagement would bring? He's one of Italy's most eligible bachelors. Everyone, and

I mean everyone, will want to know everything they can about the woman he chooses as his bride.'

'But is it wise to go to Sicily with him? I mean, you seem to have zero willpower when it comes to that man. He was your first and only one-night stand, remember? You. The girl who has to date someone like five times before you even think about kissing them, let alone sleeping with them.'

Isla was glad their phone call wasn't a video one as she could feel heat creeping into her cheeks. 'That's rich coming from the girl who doesn't even go as far as kissing a man before she rejects him out of hand.'

'You know my reasons for that,' Layla said. 'You've seen my limp and the scars on my leg. Men today have such weak stomachs.'

'One day you'll meet a man who doesn't even notice your limp and scars.'

Layla snorted. 'I stopped believing in fairy tales a long time ago. Anyway, we're not talking about me. We're talking about you. I'm worried you're going to get hurt all over again.'

'I know what I'm doing this time around. I'm not going to do anything rash.'

'Maybe on some level you do love him but don't want to admit it.'

Her feelings about Rafe were confusing to say the least. She wouldn't go as far as saying she was in love with him, but neither could she understand why her attraction to him was so powerful and irresistible. 'I'm not in love with him. In lust, maybe, but that's not enough to build a marriage on.'

'I don't know about that,' Layla said. 'It's a damn good start. Besides, a marriage of convenience can often turn into something else. It happens.'

'I thought you stopped reading fairy tales?'

'Touché,' Layla said with a little laugh. 'But seriously, Isla, you should give it some thought. You've made a baby together. It would be wonderful to be able to bring up the baby in a stable and secure home, unlike what we had growing up. And you could do a lot worse than Rafael Angeliri.'

'I know, but it's a big step and I need more time to think about it.'

Rafe had come crashing back into her life, making her feel things she didn't want to feel. The closer she got to him, the more dangerous it became. Lust often masqueraded as love and vice versa. Loving someone was too dangerous. It gave them the power to hurt you. To leave you. To reject you. She couldn't allow herself to experience the emotional devastation of her childhood all over again.

'Does he want to sleep with you?' Layla asked. 'I mean, did you get that vibe?'

'He's a hot-blooded thirty-five-year-old man. Of course, I got that vibe, but I'm going to do my best to resist him.'

'Good luck with that.'

Isla had a feeling she was going to need more than luck. She was going to need a flipping miracle.

When Rafe came back to the penthouse, Isla was standing looking out at the view of Edinburgh Castle and the Princes Street Gardens below. She turned when he came in but it was hard to read her expression.

'Weren't you worried I might do a runner?' she asked.

He shrugged one shoulder. 'I would have found you without too much trouble. Hotel management have your address.' He held up the small travel bag he was carrying. 'I took the liberty of going to your flat and picking up a few of your things. Your landlady was most obliging when I told her we are a couple.'

Her eyebrows snapped together in a frown. 'You did *what*?' Her hands balled into fists at her sides. 'You had no right to—'

'As your baby's father, I have the right to make sure your health and safety is my top priority,' Rafe said, placing the bag on the luggage rack. 'I've arranged a flight in the morning. You can spend the night here with me.'

'I'm not sleeping in that bed with you.' Her voice vibrated with fury and her eyes flashed blue streaks of lightning. 'You can't make me.'

'As much as I would love to prove you wrong, *cara*, on this occasion I will gladly relinquish my place in the bed and sleep on the sofa. You need your rest before we travel tomorrow.'

She continued to glower at him like her eyes were heat lamps. 'I want to make something perfectly clear. I'm only going to Sicily with you to rest and recuperate. Not to resume our...our fling.'

'Fine, but you will need to share my bed at my villa because I don't want my staff speculating on our relationship,' Rafe said. 'You will be there as my fiancée. That is one thing I will not compromise on. You are no longer a casual lover. You are the mother of my soon-to-be-born child.'

Her shoulders stiffened and her lips flattened. 'You think I won't be able to help myself, don't you? You think once I lie down next to you I'll be crawling all over you begging you to make love to me.'

That was exactly what Rafe thought. Trouble was, he was exactly the same. She might pretend to be immune to him but he knew her too well to buy it. And as for his own immunity to her? He had none. He was as aware of her as he had ever been—maybe even more so. 'The decision as to whether or not we resume our physical relationship will be entirely up to you.'

She spun away so her back was towards him, her arms wrapped around her body. 'How many lovers have you had since I left? Or have you lost count?' Her voice had a hoarse quality as if the question had come out against her will.

Rafe didn't see any reason to lie. 'None.'

Isla swung back around to face him, her expression etched in puzzlement. 'None? But I saw pictures of you with…' Her words and her gaze dropped away, her teeth savaging her lower lip.

He gave a rueful smile. 'I went on dates, yes. But I didn't sleep with anyone.'

Her gaze crept back up to meet his. 'But why not?'

'It didn't feel appropriate until I worked out what went wrong with us.'

A frown crinkled her smooth forehead like tiny creases in silk. 'But you've had plenty of breakups before ours. Do you normally take a time-out between flings to reflect on what went wrong?'

'Not usually, but then again I'm normally the one to end a fling and I always know exactly why I've ended it.' Mostly out of boredom and disinterest. The novelty and excitement having worn off. But it hadn't with Isla. Not one little bit.

A spark of her old feistiness lit her gaze. 'So that rankled, did it? That I got in first.'

It rankled far more than Rafe cared to admit. 'If it hadn't been for the pregnancy, would you have ended our fling when you did?'

Her eyes drifted out of reach of his and her hands made a business of straightening her clothes over her body. 'Your track record isn't great with relationships, Rafe. But then, nor is mine. We would have bored each other sooner rather than later.'

'You didn't show any signs of boredom. I haven't had a more enthusiastic lover.'

Her cheeks were tinged with a delicate shade of pink. 'It was just sex.'

'Was it?' Rafe had had plenty of 'just sex' and it had felt nothing like what they had shared during those passionate two months.

Isla moved a little further away as if she didn't trust herself around him. Rafe didn't trust himself either and had to keep a firm lid on his self-control, because all he wanted to do was prove to her how good they were together. To remind her of the scorching-hot passion that flowed so naturally between them. He could feel the pulse of it now. The crackling energy in the air tightening the atmosphere.

She flicked him a cutting glance, raising her chin in an imperious fashion. 'You only want me now because you can't have me. I've become a challenge to you.'

'And you're only resisting because we both know if I came over there and kissed you I would have you on that bed and naked within two minutes flat.'

Her gaze stayed locked on his but he could see the effort it cost her. Her body gave a tiny shudder as if she was remembering every time they had landed on a bed in a hot tangle of naked limbs. 'Don't even think about it.' Her voice sounded breathless and uneven. Her gaze slipped to his mouth, as if mentally recalling how it felt to have his lips crushed to hers.

Rafe was desperately trying not to think about it. He was getting hot and hard being in the same room as her. He had never kissed a more responsive mouth. He could still recall the pillow softness of her lips against his, the sweet milky vanilla and honey taste of her mouth, the heat and fire of her playful tongue.

Before he could stop himself, he closed the distance in slow measured strides, giving her plenty of time to move away if she wanted to. But she stayed statue-still, the ink-black circles of her pupils flaring the closer he got. Her slim throat moving up and down over a swallow, her tongue snaking out to moisten her lips. He took a handful of her luxuriant red-gold hair, watching as she momentarily closed her eyes like a cat anticipating the next sensual stroke of its master's hand. 'Tell me you don't like me touching you like this, *tesoro*.' He traced the outline of her mouth with a lazy fingertip, delighting in the way her lips parted with a soft gasp of need.

She placed her hands flat against his chest, her touch as searing as a brand, and he had to fight not to haul her closer to imprint his body on hers from pelvis to pelvis. Her fingers curled into the fabric of his shirt and she moved a fraction nearer as if compelled by a force outside of her control. The same force that was drawing his body to her like a metal filing to a magnet. He sucked in a breath as her hips came into contact with his. The blood surging to his groin, swelling, stiffening, extending. How he had missed her! Missed the feel of her supple body against him, responding to him, needing him as much as he needed her. The feverish desire rippled through him in hot waves, shooting electrifying darts around his body. He slid a hand to the base of her spine, the lush curves of her bottom so close to the edge of his hand it made it tingle. He couldn't take his eyes off her mouth. Her lips were naturally cherry-red, the top lip as full as the lower one and pushed up slightly in a cupid's bow.

'If you kiss me it will only complicate things…' Her voice was just shy of a whisper.

Rafe slid his other hand along the creamy curve of her cheek, her skin petal-soft against his palm. The need was thrumming deeply inside him like the background hum of a microwave. 'That doesn't sound like a no. I want to hear you say it. Tell me you don't want me to kiss you.'

Her eyes were luminous, shining with the same need he could feel barrelling through his body. 'Why are you doing this?' Her eyes flicked from his mouth to his gaze and back again.

Because I still want you. Rafe's hand moved in a slow glide from the base of her spine to the back of her head, sinking into the silky softness of her cloud of curls, his fingers massaging her scalp the way she had loved so much in the past. 'What am I doing, *cara*? Hmm?'

'You're making me want you.'

'And that's a bad thing?' Rafe asked, meshing his gaze with hers, his body so hard with need it made thinking difficult. He was going on instinct—primal instinct that drove his blood through his veins at breakneck speed. Swelling his tissues into a hotbed of longing that called on every bit of will-power he possessed to keep in control. Had he ever wanted a woman more than Isla? It was like a tornado in his body, rampaging through him until he could think of nothing but sinking, plunging into her tight wet warmth.

She pressed her lips together so firmly they went from red to white. But as soon as she released them they flooded with blood and he ached to cover them with his own. 'I've spent the last three months trying to forget about you, Rafe.'

Rafe sent a finger along the underside of her cheek to the base of her chin. 'Were you successful?'

Her eyelashes came down to half-mast, her hands leaving the front of his shirt to pull his head down so his mouth was within a breath of hers. 'No. Damn you. Not at all.'

He had dreamed of this moment for the last three empty and lonely months. It was all the invitation he needed. He closed the distance between their mouths and let the fireworks begin.

Isla had told herself she was prepared for Rafe to kiss her. He'd kissed her so many times before so she should have known what to expect. But as soon as his mouth came down on hers an explosion erupted in her body. Desires and needs she had almost forgotten about leapt to life like embers stirred into dancing flames and shooting and darting sparks. His lips moved against hers in a drugging kiss, slow and sensual, his hard lower body pressed against hers in such an erotic contact it made her legs unsteady. Electric pulses shot from her mouth to her pelvis, his masterful kiss tingling every cell of her flesh into throbbing life.

He deepened the kiss with a commanding stroke of his tongue against the seam of her mouth, and she opened to him like a flower opening to the first hot blast of spring sunshine. How had she survived months without this magical madness rushing through her body? How had she survived the feel of his arms around her body, holding her as if he never wanted to let her go? She wound her arms around his neck, desperate to keep his mouth clamped to hers. Desperate to feel alive again. Desperate to feel the storm of ferocious attraction pounding from his mouth to hers.

No one kissed her like Rafe did. His kiss was like a potent drug she had lived too long without. Now she had tasted his lips again, she was addicted all over again. Powerfully, dangerously addicted. His lips continued their sensual exploration, his tongue dancing with hers with such exquisite and mesmerising choreography it caused a swooping sensation in her stomach. Isla pressed herself closer, more than a little shocked at the sounds of pleasure and encouragement she was making but unable to stop herself. She wanted this. She wanted *him*. She had never stopped wanting him.

His hand came up to cradle one side of her face, the other pressing in the small of her back, holding her close against his growing erection. Feeling the extension of his body, his unmistakable desire for her, feeling *him*, ramped up her own need until she was practically grinding her pelvis against him to get closer.

His hand slid up to her hair, his fingers splayed at first and then clutching at the strands with just the right amount of tension. The sort of tension that made every hair on her head shiver at the roots, every cell in her body shudder in reaction and her self-control roll over and play dead. How could she resist this man? How could she resist the feelings he and he alone evoked in her? Passion hot and strong and irresistible. Passion that made her forget about everything but the biological need of their bodies. The passionate need to unite their bodies in the most primal way of all to trigger a tumultuous storm of blissful release.

Suddenly the kiss was over.

Rafe pulled away from her as if a director on a movie set had suddenly called 'cut'. His expression was masked, although his eyes were bright and his pupils wide as bottomless black pools. 'So, at least that's something that hasn't changed.' The was a note of triumph in his voice that made her wish she hadn't been so responsive. So transparent. So wanton. *Again.* Why did she have zero resistance to him? Why?

Isla moved a few steps away, swishing her hair over one shoulder in a gesture of nonchalance she was nowhere near feeling. 'What time are we leaving tomorrow?' A subject change was her only way of restoring some of her dignity. She couldn't help feeling he had engineered that little kissing session to prove he had the upper hand when it came to self-control. But hadn't she always been out of her league where he was concerned? He was sophisticated and suave and she was riddled with shameful secrets.

'Mid-morning. I've allowed some time for you to sleep in.'

She sent him a spearing glance. 'Alone?'

A dark gleam entered his gaze. 'I will leave that up to you to decide.'

CHAPTER FOUR

ISLA WOKE EARLY the next morning to find the space beside her in the bed hadn't been slept in. The sheets were smooth and crease-free, the pillows showing no indentation of Rafe's head ever having rested there. Had he gone out? She had been so tired she hadn't registered any sound of him coming or going in the suite once she'd closed her eyes the night before.

She got out of bed and padded out to the sitting room of the suite and found Rafe asleep in one of the sofa chairs, his long legs stretched out in front of him and crossed at the ankles. He looked a bit worse for wear—his shirt was open to the middle of his chest and crumpled and half out of one side of his trousers. His jaw was richly peppered with dark regrowth and his hair was tousled as if his hands had gone through it a few times. There was a book, open and face down on the floor, as if it had tumbled from his lap while he had drifted off to sleep.

Isla was reluctant to disturb him but she felt a twinge of guilt that he had spent the night sleeping in a chair rather than share the bed with her. His gallantry was not only unexpected but strangely touching.

He suddenly opened his eyes as if he sensed her looking at him. He uncrossed his ankles and pulled his legs back closer to the chair and ran a hand over his face, the sound of his palm moving across his stubble loud in the silence.

'How did you sleep?' He smothered a yawn and stood and stretched his lower back by placing his hands on his hips and leaning backwards slightly, not quite disguising a wince.

'Clearly a bit better than you,' Isla said. 'Why didn't you come to bed?'

He dropped his hands back by his sides and gave her a rueful smile that made something in her chest ping. 'I didn't trust myself to keep my hands off you.'

Isla felt betraying warmth spreading through her cheeks so bent to pick up his book rather than encounter his gaze. She hadn't trusted herself not to drift into old habits—reaching for him in the middle of the night, snuggling up against his back, her arms around his waist, her legs entangling with his. Her hands exploring his… She snapped the book closed and placed it on the nearest surface. 'I'm sorry you had such an uncomfortable night. I was so tired I probably wouldn't have noticed if you had joined me.'

'Wouldn't you?' His eyes met hers in a challenging lock that made her inner core contract.

The silence seemed to buzz with a host of erotic memories.

Isla couldn't stop her gaze from drifting to his mouth, her tongue sneaking out to moisten her suddenly parchment-dry lips. She was aware of him following the betraying movement, his eyes darkly hooded, the subtle change in his breathing signalling his own attraction. She brought her gaze back up to his. 'You don't strike me as the sort of man to touch a woman when she's expressly told you not to.' Her tone fell a little short of starchy schoolmistress and leaned more towards *I want you to kiss me.*

Rafe came over to her and tucked a wayward corkscrew curl back behind her ear. His touch was light and tender and it made every cell in her body cry out for more. He knew all her pleasure spots, all her erogenous zones, all her vulnerabilities. All her needs. And how pathetic her self-control. 'I would find it a lot easier not to touch you if I didn't think you wanted me. But you do, don't you, *cara*? You haven't forgotten how good we were together, *si*?'

His hand cupped her cheek as if he were cradling a ripe peach he was trying not to bruise, his thumb moving back and forth in a slow caress. Isla couldn't disguise her delicate shiver of reaction in time. She placed her hand on his wrist, fully intending to push him away, but instead her fingers curled around the tanned strength of his arm. His skin was warm and the black masculine hairs on his wrist tickled against her skin. His eyes were as dark and mysterious as a deep forest, flecks of leaf litter brown and lichen green fringed with ink-black lashes framed by prominent eyebrows above.

'This is like a game to you, isn't it?' Her voice didn't come out quite as reproving as she would have liked.

'The fact that you're carrying my child is not a game to me, Isla.' His tone had a deep note of gravitas and a frown pulled at his forehead. 'Nor is the fact that we still feel something for each other.'

This time she managed to summon enough will-power to step back from him. She folded her arms across her body, sending him a cool stare. 'If I wasn't pregnant and we'd run into each other again, would you have offered me what you're offering now?'

Something flickered at the back of his gaze. He gave a rough-edged sigh and pushed a hand through the thickness of his hair. 'An affair maybe, but probably not marriage.'

'So, I was fling material but not wife material.' Isla didn't say it as a question but as a statement. A confirmation of all she believed about herself. Beliefs that had been reinforced throughout her childhood.

You're not good enough.

'Marriage wasn't something I was actively seeking,' Rafe said. 'But things are different now.'

'But I'm not different. I'm the same person I was five months ago.'

His eyes cruised over her abdomen. 'Not quite the same, *mio piccolo*. You are pregnant with my child. That is a game-changer.'

A few hours later, they arrived at Rafe's Liberty style villa situated in the borough of Mondello in Sicily, the site of a popular white sand beach. In spite of her travel weariness and conflicted feelings about coming with Rafe to his home, Isla couldn't help feeling thrilled to be back where she had spent some of the happiest weeks of her life. Their time together here had shown her a world she had never been part of before. A world she had barely realised existed. Not just the glamour and riches he took for granted, but the sensual world of his lovemaking. She had spent her days sketching and painting or exploring the sites while Rafe worked, and then in the evenings he had devoted his entire attention to her. And the last couple of weeks Rafe hadn't worked at all. He'd cancelled all his engagements and spent the whole time with her. No one had ever made her feel so special, so desired, so fulfilled.

However, the sensual idyll had been slightly tainted for her by the presence of Rafe's housekeeper, Concetta. Isla had never been able to relate to the older woman, who seemed to wear a perpetual frown of disapproval but, interestingly, only when Rafe wasn't around. Isla found her sly and surly and sneering but Rafe would never hear a bad word about her. Isla had tried to talk to him a couple of times about his housekeeper's behaviour towards her but he'd always laughed off her concerns and told her Concetta was old-school Sicilian—a little guarded and formal with newcomers. On reflection, Isla wondered if he couldn't be bothered back then to do anything about Concetta's behaviour because he knew his relationship with her had an end point, as all his relationships had in the past.

How would the housekeeper take the news of Isla's pregnancy? Had Rafe told her? And how would she react to the news of Rafe's intention to marry the mother of his child?

'Do you still have Concetta working for you?' Isla asked once they had entered the refreshingly cool foyer of the villa.

'*Sì*, I am still here. He hasn't fired me yet but who knows?' the housekeeper said, approaching from further inside the villa. Concetta was a spritely woman in her late fifties who moved as quickly and efficiently as her acerbic tongue. She had black button eyes and weathered features and wiry salt and pepper hair pulled back tightly into a bun at the back of her head. Isla had never seen a hair out of place on the housekeeper's head and suspected not one strand would dare to escape its rigid confines. Concetta was dressed all in black and her deep frown reminded Isla of a pernickety schoolmistress about to dress down a recalcitrant pupil. And eagerly looking forward to it.

'It's nice to see you again,' Isla said, trying to inject some authenticity into her tone.

'Hmph.' Concetta swept her gaze over Isla's swollen belly, her thin lips pursing. She swung her gaze to Rafe. 'Are you sure it's yours?'

Rafe's mouth tightened and he spoke to the housekeeper in a rich Sicilian dialect that Isla couldn't understand. But the message was loud and clear, for Concetta raised her eyebrows and, with another insolent flash of her gaze at Isla, turned and stalked out in the direction of the kitchen, further inside the villa. Even the sound of her retreating footsteps seemed to contain an insulting rhythm. I. Will. Get. You. For. This.

'I'm sorry,' Rafe said, turning back to Isla. 'Concetta can be a bit difficult but she'll soften up over time. Our news has been a shock to her, that's all.'

Isla arched a sceptical eyebrow. 'And you want to marry me? Seriously? I can't see her accepting me as your wife any time soon. She's never liked me. Not that you listened when I tried to tell you how awful she was to me at times. I can only imagine what juicy insults she'll save for me when you're not around.'

His expression hardened and he closed the front door with a definitive *clunk*. 'She will have to accept you or find some other employment.'

Isla folded her arms and cocked her head. 'Tell me something… Was she rude to all your other lovers?

No wonder your relationships only lasted a matter of a week or two.'

Rafe's gaze shifted away and he shrugged off his lightweight jacket and hung it on a black wrought iron coat stand. 'I haven't brought anyone here before you. I mostly hooked up when I was away on business. It made it less…complicated.'

Isla stared at him in shock. 'What? No one? No one at all?'

He turned with an unreadable expression on his face. 'This is my home. My private sanctuary. I don't like sharing it with strangers.'

'Nor, apparently, does your housekeeper.' Isla's tone was deliberately wry to disguise how unsettled she was by his revelation about his past. What did it mean? Why had he brought *her* here? What had it been about her that had made him relax his rules and have her stay for almost two months as his live-in lover?

An enigmatic smile suddenly tilted one side of his mouth. 'I know what you're thinking.'

Isla did her best to keep her expression neutral. 'Oh? Do tell.'

He came to stand in front of her, close enough to tuck a wayward curl back behind her ear. His touch sent a wave of shuddery longing through her and it was all she could do to stand there as still as one of the marble statues in the grand foyer. His hazel eyes roamed her features, lingering for a pulsing moment on her mouth. The atmosphere became charged with electricity—a pulsing energy that made every pore of her skin lift in heightened awareness.

'You're wondering why I brought you here, *sì*? Why you and no one else.' His voice was low and deep, a gravel and honey combo that made the base of her spine tingle like fine sand was trickling between her vertebrae.

Isla glanced at his mouth and disguised a swallow. His fingers found another tendril of hair but this time he wound it around his finger, gently tethering her to him. A silken bond that made her scalp prickle with delight and her inner core tug and tighten.

'I know one thing for sure—it wasn't because you fell madly in love with me.' She aimed for a light tone but somehow ended up sounding bitter.

A small frown tugged at his forehead and he slowly unwound her hair from his finger, tucking it behind her ear as he had done previously. 'No. It wasn't that... But then you weren't in love with me, or has that changed in the last few months?'

Isla screened her expression with cool indifference. An indifference she was not so sure she felt. Had ever felt. She wouldn't go as far as saying she was in love with him—it was too threatening to lower her guard to that degree. Loving someone gave them the power to hurt you and hadn't she been hurt enough? 'Of course not. No offence or anything. I'm sure plenty of women before me have fallen deeply in love with you and paid the price for doing so.'

His eyes moved back and forth between each of hers as if looking for something screened behind her gaze. 'One of the reasons I brought you here was to avoid the press. I wanted to enjoy being with you without a bunch of cameras following us all the time.'

'And the other reason?'

He gave another mercurial half-smile. 'Put it down to a moment of weakness on my part.' He stepped back from her and picked up her bag he'd brought in earlier. 'You should rest for a bit. It's been a long day.'

Isla followed him to the master bedroom, a strange sense of déjà vu assailing her as she entered the suite. She could recall in intricate detail the first time she had come into this bedroom with him. And the explosive passion they had shared on that massive bed moments later. She sent Rafe a surreptitious glance to see if he was showing any signs of being affected by memories of the past but his expression was inscrutable. So impersonally inscrutable he could have been a butler showing a low-status houseguest to their room.

The room contained the light but intoxicating citrus notes of his aftershave and the smell of freshly laundered bedlinen. The windows overlooking the estate were open, the sheer silk curtains billowing like sails.

'Are you cold? I can close these if you'd like.' Rafe gestured to the windows.

'I'm fine. Leave them open. It's nice to have some fresh air after being on the plane.' Isla placed her tote bag on a velvet chair, doing her best to keep her eyes away from the bed.

'I'll get Concetta to bring you up some refreshment.'

She swung back around to look at him. 'Please don't. I'd…I'd like to be alone for a while.' Her gaze fell away and she bit down on her lower lip. The last thing she needed right now was a hail of insults from Rafe's unfriendly housekeeper. Her emotions were all over the place as it was. Coming back here had stirred them into a writhing nest of anguish.

She was uncertain of how she should handle Rafe's proposal. Uncertain of her place in his life, even if she *had* a place in his life other than as the mother of his child. A child he might well be able to take off her if he put his mind to it. She didn't belong in his world and coming back here only reinforced it. She was a fish so far out of the safety of water she was choking, gasping. It would be foolish of her to let her guard down. She had let her guard down in the past and ended up bitterly disappointed each and every time. After her mother died, she'd hoped her father would claim her but he had handed her back into the foster system as soon as he could. Then there was the disappointment of family after family showing an interest in her, meetings arranged and then suddenly cancelled. Her hopes shattered time and time again. Even her past two boyfriends—men she'd thought she had a future with—had dumped her without ceremony.

Was she cursed always to have people leave her?

Rafe came over to her and took both her hands in his. His gaze softened and his hands gently squeezed hers. 'Are you feeling unwell? Nauseous?'

Isla kept her gaze averted, looking instead at her hands encased in the warm strong shelter of his. 'No. Just…tired.' Overwhelmed. Out of place. Worried. Vulnerable.

He nudged up her chin with his finger to mesh his gaze with hers. 'I know this is a big step for you, coming back here with me. But we have to focus on what's best for the baby. *Our* baby.'

Isla slipped out of his hold and put some distance between them, her arms going around her middle. 'Your housekeeper doesn't even think it is your baby.'

Rafe let out a rough-edged sigh and rubbed a hand over his face. 'Do you want me to get rid of her? Is that what you want? To dismiss her and find someone else? Concetta has only ever worked for me. Her life hasn't been easy. She was married to a brute of a man who left her penniless after she finally worked up the courage to leave him. She has no other skills.'

There was a part of Isla that wanted exactly that— for him to terminate the housekeeper's employment right then and there. But there was another part of her that knew how it felt to be dismissed from a much-needed job for speaking her mind too freely. Knew how it felt to be let go. Dismissed. Rejected. 'No. That's not what I want,' Isla said, turning her back to him. 'I can stand up for myself. I've had to do it most of my life. God knows no one else was going to do it for me.'

Rafe came up behind her and placed his hands on the tops of her shoulders and turned her to face him. His expression was etched in a frown. 'What was your family's reaction to the news of your pregnancy? Were they happy for you?'

Ah, the sticky web we weave...

Isla went to duck out of his hold but his grip tightened on her shoulders.

'No,' he said, his frown deepening. 'Don't run away. Talk to me.'

Isla couldn't meet his gaze and focused on the tanned column of his throat instead. 'I don't have a family. My mother died of alcohol poisoning when I was seven. I was handed to my father, who'd been divorced from my mother since I was five, but he didn't keep me for long. I spent the rest of my childhood in foster care.'

The sound of Rafe's sharply indrawn breath brought her gaze back up to his. 'Why didn't you tell me before?' he asked. 'Why give me the impression you had a normal childhood?'

This time Isla was successful in extricating herself from his hold. She cupped her elbows in her crossed over hands, keeping her expression guarded. 'Because it was easier than explaining. You didn't talk about your family either and I was okay with that. We were having a fling, Rafe. Not promising to share our lives for ever.'

'Was anything you told me about yourself true? Anything at all?'

Isla sat on the end of the bed before her legs gave way out of sheer exhaustion. Emotional exhaustion more than anything. The only person who knew about her childhood was her friend Layla because they had met in foster care. But Layla had been lucky enough to be claimed by her great-aunt, who took her to live with her at her place of employment as housekeeper for a wealthy Scottish family. 'I'm sorry but I don't like talking about my background. I try to forget it as much as possible.'

He came to hunker down in front of her, one of his hands coming to rest on her knee. 'What did you think I was going to say if you had told me?'

Isla affected a light ironic laugh. 'I can tell you one thing—you wouldn't have invited me back here to live with you for two months. You date supermodels and starlets, not girls from a Scottish slum.'

His eyes searched hers for a moment. 'You seriously think I wouldn't have become involved with you because of your background? You think I'm that much of a snob?'

Isla inched up her chin, pride her only reliable armour. 'Why would you? We have nothing in common. You grew up with money. I grew up in poverty. You have a mother and a father and siblings. I have no one.'

A shadow of something passed over his face and he got to his feet like he had suddenly morphed into a tired old man. He pushed a hand through his hair, leaving deep finger comb marks. It seemed an age before he spoke.

'My father's wife is not my mother. And my brothers are only half-siblings. My mother died when I was fourteen. She was my father's mistress.'

Isla's eyes rounded. 'But everything I've read in the press about your background—'

'Was fabricated by my father to whitewash his reputation,' Rafe said with an unmistakable note of bitterness in his tone. 'He kept his two lives separate until he had an almost fatal car accident when I was thirteen. We didn't question why he was always travelling for business—it was his job. He provided for us, took us on nice holidays, showered us with gifts. We didn't even question why he couldn't spend Christmas with us every year. There was always a crisis he had to attend to, staffing problems or whatever that only he could fix. When it looked like he might not make it through the night, someone from his company phoned my mother and we rushed to the hospital to find him surrounded by his family. His first family. His *official* family.'

Isla rose from the bed and went to him, touching him on the forearm. 'It must have been awful finding out like that.'

'It was.' The two words were as sharp and brutal as slash marks on tender flesh.

Her arm fell away from his. 'You said your mother died when you were fourteen. Did you live with your father and his…other family after that?'

A cruel smile twisted his mouth. 'No. I was sent to boarding school. In England. Far enough away so I didn't disturb my father's happy little nest.'

'It can't have been too happy a nest if your father felt the need to have a mistress for all those years,' Isla said, frowning.

'My father's wife came from money. Lots of money. A divorce was out of the question. She gave him an ultimatum once he recovered from the accident—ditch his mistress and keep his distance from me. So he did.'

'What? He dumped you both just like that?' Isla snapped her fingers for effect.

Rafe's eyes were as hard and cold as marble. 'His company would have collapsed without Elena's steady injection of funds. Money was always going to win over sentiment with my father.'

'Have you any contact with him now?'

'Minimal.' Rafe straightened one of the original artworks on the wall with a minuscule adjustment. He turned to look at her and added, 'It's funny, but my father and his wife find it far less distasteful to include me in their happy family game now I have become one of the wealthiest men in Sicily.'

'I don't know how you can have anything to do with them after the way you and your mum were treated,' Isla said.

'My half-brothers are decent men. It's not their fault our father is a weak man whose primary motivation is greed.'

'But you loved him once? Your father, I mean.'

Rafe's mouth turned down at the corners and another shadow passed over his face. 'I idolised him. He was my hero, the person I most looked up to. For years I modelled myself on him.' He made a harsh sound of disgust at the back of his throat. 'But everything he told me was lies.'

And Isla had done the same. Guilt crawled over her like a spreading stain and she could feel its hot colour blooming in her cheeks. She had lied by omission rather than blatantly telling mistruths. She was still doing it, withholding information—for how could she tell him about the photos? The shameful shots of her in that gentleman's bar. Her young nubile body flagrantly exposed. Photos that would be circulated for large sums of money if she were ever to marry Rafe. She knew how much he hated the intrusion of the press. Trailer trash to marry one of Sicily's richest men? Of course, it would cause a storm of avid interest. Rafe's housekeeper wouldn't be the only person in his life who would be throwing nasty insults at her—the whole world would do so.

'I'm sorry you've had such a difficult time,' Isla said. 'But you must feel some sense of satisfaction that you made it on your own?'

A fleeting smile touched his mouth. 'Like you, *si*?'

She gave one of her pretend laughs. 'I've hardly made it, Rafe. I haven't touched a paintbrush in three months.'

'Then we will have to do something about that. I have organised for us to visit my grandmother in a couple of days. She lives in Marsala, about eighty kilometres from here.'

'You didn't mention anything about her when I was here last. Why?'

His expression became shuttered. 'My *nonna* is old-school, like Concetta. She disapproves of casual relationships. She's been waiting for years for me to settle down. The time is right now for you to meet her as my fiancée.'

There was that annoying F word again. Fiancée. And what was his old-school *nonna* going to think of Isla's topless photos if they were to go public? It didn't bear thinking about.

'I haven't said I was going to marry you, Rafe.'

He pulled back the bed covers and patted the bed,

his gaze giving nothing away. 'Have a rest now, *cara*. I insist. You look tired and a little flushed.'

Isla slipped off her shoes and lay down on the cloud-soft bed and he pulled the cool sheet back over her, leaning down to press a soft-as-air kiss to the middle of her forehead. The surprising tenderness of the kiss made her wonder if somewhere deep inside him he actually cared a little for her. Not just for the baby she was carrying but for *her*. Was she being foolish to hope? Hadn't she learned her lesson by now about harbouring vain hopes? He was a good man, a caring man, with perhaps more sensitivity than she had given him credit for in the past. Surely his treatment of his housekeeper proved that he had a heart. But would he ever open it enough to welcome Isla in?

He was almost to the door before she found her voice. 'Rafe?'

He turned to look at her. 'Yes?'

Isla chewed at her lower lip. 'But what if, like Concetta, your grandmother doesn't accept me?'

A determined light appeared in his green and brown gaze. 'Once you are wearing my ring, she will accept you. Concetta too. Now rest.'

If only he knew how far from acceptable she felt.

CHAPTER FIVE

RAFE SAT IN his study at his desk and flicked his gold pen back and forth. He had business matters to see to—emails to send, documents to sign, deals to negotiate—but for once in his life he didn't feel like working. He felt like walking back upstairs and joining Isla in his bed.

That was where he wanted to be right now. With his arms around her, kissing her until she moaned, touching her until she begged. Burying himself in her sweet hot warmth and forgetting about everything but how good they were together.

Better than good—the best.

He should be angry with her for not telling him about her background. He should be feeling blindsided and betrayed, but somehow he wasn't. Instead, he felt compassion for her. Deep compassion. The circumstances of her childhood were terrible and it pained him she hadn't felt comfortable telling him when they were having a fling.

Bringing her back here to his villa had opened

up a vault of memories. A vault he had kept tightly locked. When she'd left him three months ago, he had ruthlessly disciplined himself *not* to think about their time together. Every time his mind would drift to the scent of her skin, the softness of her mouth, the creamy perfection of her breasts, he would throw himself into work or do a punishing, muscle-burning workout. He hadn't allowed himself to dwell on what he was missing. Not just the hot sex and lively conversations—he'd had plenty of hot sex and lively conversations before. It was Isla he'd missed. Her smile, her tinkling bell-like laugh, her silken touch on his skin.

Dio, her touch on his skin. He ached to feel it again. Ached and throbbed to bury himself in her and send them both to paradise.

Concetta had questioned on numerous occasions why he insisted on keeping Isla's things in the walk-in wardrobe but he had expressly forbidden his housekeeper to remove them. Every time he went to his wardrobe and was confronted with Isla's clothes it was a form of self-torture. Things he had bought her. It was inconsistent of him to keep them there, as he'd been trying *not* to think about her, and yet he had kept them there to remind himself of his failure to read the signs on their relationship. Failure was a word he loathed and nothing reeked of abject failure more than to be blindsided in a relationship. Her presence in his villa had changed the atmosphere from the moment she had stepped over the threshold.

And it had changed it again now.

Rafe tossed his pen aside and rose to go to the windows that looked out over the stunning white sand–fringed beach of Mondello below. His villa, with its private gardens and infinity pool overlooking the ocean, was his castle. His fortress. The home he wished his mother had lived long enough to see. To enjoy with him. Years of her life had been spent living a lie and it churned his guts to think of all the things she'd done without because his father had kept her in limbo, feeding her empty promises year after year. Unlike Rafe, his mother had always known about Tino Angeliri's wife but had put up with being his mistress because she had loved him so much. And Rafe had loved him too. Deeply. And he had thought his father loved him but that was another lie. For a time, Rafe had been angry at his mother for not telling him the truth about his father earlier, but over time he'd come to realise she had only wanted to protect him.

Rafe and his mother had lived in a nice enough apartment—paid for by his father—but the one thing his mother had longed for was a garden. So Rafe had spent a veritable fortune on the garden here to honour her wish. Years of living out of his various hotels had made him appreciate this private sanctuary all the more. He had a handful of staff but mostly he was here alone.

But not now.

Isla was here and he wanted her to stay. Indefinitely. They would be parents in four months' time. He wanted his child to experience what he hadn't— legitimacy. Yes, it was old-fashioned of him in this day and age to insist on the formality of marriage. But he would settle for nothing less. He would not have Isla referred to as his mistress. He would not have his child called a love-child. He would not have his child called a bastard. He would not be a part-time parent like his father. He and Isla would be a family and he would do everything in his power to make it work.

Rafe opened the window and the salty tang of the sea breeze wafted past his nostrils. It had shocked him to find out Isla had grown up without a loving family, especially when she'd hinted at the opposite. But, looking back with the benefit of hindsight, there had been clues if he had taken the time to notice them. Isla had never called anyone on her phone in his presence. And no one had called her, apart from her friend Layla.

Not that he could talk. He didn't call his father or stepmother or half-brothers and only sent a text for birthdays. The only family member he called occasionally was his grandmother, because she was his last link to his mother. But even that relationship was tricky to handle. The shame of having a daughter 'living in sin' and having an illegitimate son by her

married lover had caused a rift between his grandmother and his mother that had meant Rafe hadn't
met his *nonna* until after his mother's death. It was
hardly the way to build a close family bond.

Rafe sighed and turned away from the window
and rubbed a hand over the back of his tense neck.
Maybe there was something fatalistic about the way
he and Isla had met in that bar in Rome. Perhaps they
had recognised something in each other—a sense of
isolation. A sense of not really belonging to anyone.
He had noticed her the moment he'd walked into
the bar. She'd been sitting in a quiet corner with a
sketchpad on her lap, her beautiful features frowning with concentration as she drew a sketch of one of
the patrons. The likeness was astonishing and Rafe
had struck up a conversation and…well, the rest was
smoking-hot history as they say. One drink and forty-
two minutes later he had her back at his hotel and in
his bed. The sex had been so phenomenal he had—
uncharacteristically for him—impulsively asked her
to come with him on a business trip to Paris. After
Paris, for the next month he took her everywhere
with him: Berlin, Zurich, Prague, Vienna, Amster-
dam, Athens and Copenhagen.

And then, even more uncharacteristic of him—
home to Sicily.

But, if he were honest with himself, it wasn't just
the sex that had made him spirit her away to his private sanctuary. He'd wanted her to himself. The more

time he'd spent with her, the more he'd realised she was different from his other casual lovers. He had taken lovers on business trips and holidays before but by the end of the trip he couldn't wait to end the fling.

But not with Isla.

He had wanted one month with her, then two, and then without notice she'd gone.

Rafe sat back down at his desk, a frown pulling at his brow. Had it been the difference in their backgrounds that had made her bolt as soon as she'd discovered she was pregnant? He clenched his right hand into a fist until his knuckles whitened. Why hadn't he tried harder to find her? Why had he allowed his pride to get in the way? He had wasted three months of valuable time, and if he hadn't by chance run into her he might never have found out about his child. And who could blame her for wanting to keep quiet about the pregnancy? He had made it clear their fling was temporary. He had made no promises. He had made no commitment other than to insist their fling was to be exclusive for its duration.

Marriage was the only way to make it up to her. The security of a formal relationship in which to bring up their child was the way forward.

The *only* way forward.

Isla woke from a surprisingly refreshing nap and sat up and pushed her tousled hair away from her face. The bright afternoon light had faded to the pastel hues of sunset, giving the room a muted and calming glow. She tossed the sheet covering her to one side and got to her feet, waiting for a moment to make sure she wasn't feeling faint. Once she was sure she was feeling fine, she went to the luxuriously appointed bathroom and did what she could to freshen up. She toyed with the idea of a shower but didn't want to chance Rafe coming in on her. Even glancing at the shower recess made something in her belly flutter. The erotic memories of what he had done to her in there flooded her brain and sent a wave of longing through her body.

She came back out to the bedroom and glanced in the direction of the walk-in wardrobe. Had he really kept all of her things? She had only taken the things she had brought with her on her trip abroad. Everything he had bought her she had left behind. She hadn't wanted any accusations of gold-digging cast her way by either him or his surly housekeeper.

She slid back the pocket doors and entered the wardrobe and something tripped in her stomach. Her clothes were neatly hanging on the opposite side to his. Her shoes arranged in tidy rows, the jewellery he'd bought her in the drawer of the glass-topped cabinet. She trailed her fingers along the row of silk and chiffon and satin articles of clothing. She opened one of the drawers below the jewellery display cabinet and found all the sexy lingerie she had once worn for him—exquisite lace and satin in an array of colours: black, red, midnight blue, hot pink and virginal white.

Isla picked up a dark blue silk and lace-trimmed camisole and matching knickers, running the gorgeous fabric through her fingers, mentally recalling the way Rafe had removed them from her body inch by inch, leaving a blazing trail of searing kisses on her exposed and quivering in anticipation flesh. She shivered and put the camisole and knickers back and shut the drawer with a snap.

But it wasn't so easy to lock away the memories of his touch.

Isla heard the door of the bedroom opening and she came out of the wardrobe to see Rafe coming into the suite carrying a long tall glass of freshly squeezed orange juice. She suddenly felt embarrassed to be found checking out the left-behind loot, so to speak. 'I'm not sure any of those things will fit me for too much longer.'

He set the juice down on the bedside table. 'Then I will buy you things that will.'

'You don't have to do that. I can buy my own clothes.' A remnant of pride sharpened her tone.

Rafe came over to her and took her hands in his. 'Did you get out of the wrong side of the bed?'

Isla pushed her lips forward in a pout. 'Not the wrong side—the wrong bed.'

His jaw tightened as if he was grinding his molars. 'I want you in my bed, Isla. It's where you belong.' The unmistakable note of authority in his voice made her all the more determined to defy him. To prove she still had some willpower where he was concerned. Some, not a lot. But some.

Her chin came up to a combative height and a surge of energy coursed through her. 'You think we can simply pick up where we left off? Get real, Rafe.'

His hands released hers to hold her by the hips instead. Isla knew she should try and get out of his hold but somehow her willpower had completely deserted her. His touch was like fire even through the layers of her clothes.

'I'll tell you what's real. This.' He brought his mouth down to just a breath away from hers. 'You can feel it, can't you?'

Isla couldn't stop her body from moving closer to his—as though it was programmed like a mobile robot going back to base for a much-needed charge. The hot hard heat of his arousal and the yearning ache of her pelvis coming into contact sent a zapping bolt of electricity through her body. Her mouth was suddenly fused to his but she didn't know who had closed the final distance. It didn't matter. All that mattered was the feeling of his lips moving with such masterful expertise on her own, feeling the commanding thrust of his tongue calling hers into sensual play. Feeling the need spiralling through her flesh, lighting up all her erogenous zones into a state of anticipatory awareness.

Isla wound her arms around his neck, her hands grasping handfuls of his hair in case he changed his mind and stepped away. She would *die* if he stepped away. A desperate moan of approval escaped her lips and she pressed closer, rubbing up against his erection, the urge to have him inside her so intense it was overwhelming.

His mouth continued its bone-melting exploration, his lips soft one minute, hard and insistent the next. His tongue darted and danced with hers in an erotic choreography that made her legs weaken, her spine tingle, her heart race. The slight graze of his stubble on her face as he changed position stirred her senses into overdrive. He took her lower lip between the gentle press of his teeth—a sexy nip and tug that sent a shower of fizzing fireworks to her core.

Isla took his lower lip between her teeth, tugging and releasing and then salving it with a slow sweep of her tongue. He shuddered and made a rough sound at the back of his throat and pulled her hard against him, one of his hands firm on the base of her spine.

'You make me crazy for you without even trying.' Rafe's voice had a desperate edge and his mouth came back down and covered hers in a searing kiss that made her need for him pummel harder through her body.

One of his hands glided underneath her top to gently cup her breast and she groaned in delight. Her breasts were even more sensitive than three months ago but her flesh recognised his touch and responded with excited fervour. He deftly unclipped her bra and brought his mouth down her naked breast, his tongue like the expert stroke of an artist's brush across her skin, around her tightly budded nipple, along the underside and back again. It was torture and yet tantalising, every nerve in her breast dancing in frenzied excitement, her inner core liquefying into molten heat.

Isla's hands went to the waistband of his trousers, fumbling with the fastening in her haste to uncover him. She needed to touch him. To taste him. To torture him the way he was torturing her. But he moved her hand away and walked her backwards to the bed, laying her down and coming down beside her, his hand continuing its frisson-inducing glide over her naked breast.

'I want you…' She was shocked at how desperate she sounded but was beyond caring. She didn't need her pride right now—what she needed was pleasure. Mind-blowing pleasure that only he could deliver. 'Please, Rafe. *Please*…' She writhed as he brought his hand to her mound, cupping her through her clothes with just enough pressure to make her arch her spine.

'Are you sure you want this?' His voice was calm and even and yet she could see the naked desire glittering in his gaze.

'Yes. A thousand times yes. You know I want you.

You want me too.' Isla pulled his head down so he would kiss her again.

He covered her mouth in a long, spine-tingling kiss, his hand going under her elastic-waisted skirt and to her knickers. He peeled them down and she bucked and writhed so she could be rid of them. She wanted no barriers between their bodies. She needed him *now*. His fingers explored her feminine folds, caressing and teasing her into throbbing excitement. She was so close. So close. *So desperately close...*

Rafe moved down her body, placing his mouth where his fingers had been caressing, using his tongue to send her over the edge into oblivion. The sensations rippled through her sensitive flesh and Isla was swept up into a cataclysmic orgasm that seemed to involve every muscle and sinew in her body. She arched, she writhed, she bucked under the exquisite ministrations of his tongue. She cried out loud—whimpering, breathless cries as her flesh rippled and ricocheted with intense pleasure.

She came back to her senses with a shuddering sigh, her eyes seeking Rafe's with sudden shyness. 'You certainly haven't lost your touch.' She reached for his hand and interlaced her fingers with his, but she sensed a guardedness in him. A pulling away even though they were holding hands, his lazy smile at odds with the mask-like expression in his gaze.

'Nor you,' he said, leaning forward to press a light kiss to her forehead.

Isla frowned in confusion, doubts creeping in like shadows under a door. Why wasn't he continuing? Why wasn't he as desperate for release as she had been just moments ago? Or was he trying to prove a point? She was the one who needed him more than he needed her. 'Aren't you going to finish—?'

'Not right now.' He moved off the bed with athletic grace, standing beside it to look down at her. If he had constructed a brick wall between them it couldn't have been any more obvious that he was done here. Done with *her*. 'Concetta will have dinner ready shortly. Why don't you shower and change and I'll meet you downstairs?'

Isla launched herself off the bed, scrabbling at her clothes to put them in some sort of order. 'Why don't you stop telling me what to do?' she shot back, stung by his rejection. Stung with the pain of being discarded like a plaything that had lost its appeal.

A line of tension rippled along the length of his jaw and turned his eyes to stone. 'I am merely trying to do the right thing by you, Isla. You've had a long and exhausting day.'

'Is it my pregnancy that's a turn-off for you? You're feeling a little squeamish about making love to—'

'No.'

'Then what? Five months ago we would have been onto our second orgasm by now.' Possibly her third or fourth.

Rafe tucked his shirt back into his trousers and then raked his hand through his hair. 'We rushed into our relationship in the past. I'd like to take things a little more slowly this time around.'

Isla let out an unladylike curse. 'Why? So you can make me fall in love with you so I won't be able to say no to your offer of marriage? Not going to happen, buddy. No flipping way.' She spun away and stalked to the bathroom, furious with him—furious with herself for not resisting him. She slammed the door and leaned back against it. Why had she fallen into his arms like a wanton, desperate woman? She had gone up in flames and he had been in total control, not once being tempted beyond his endurance. What did that say about their relationship? It said it was out of balance. The power dynamic put her at a distinct disadvantage.

But hadn't it always?

His world. Her world. And never the twain shall meet.

But their worlds had collided with the conception of a child. A baby who could bridge the chasm as nothing else could. Could she settle for such a compromise when all her life she had wanted to be loved for herself?

Rafe knocked on the bathroom door. 'Isla. Open up.' His tone contained a warning note.

'Go away.' Isla glared at her reflection, ashamed of herself for being so weak. 'I *hate* you.'

His mocking laugh made her want to throw every cosmetic jar on the marble bathroom counter at the door. Smash. Smash. Smash. Then she would write a rude word all over the mirror in red lipstick and on the snowy white towels—every single one of them. She clenched her hands into fists, fighting the urge to scream with frustration, but instead a broken sob came from nowhere and she bent her head and clasped her face in her hands, her shoulders shaking with the effort of keeping her emotions in check.

The door suddenly clicked open and Rafe stepped inside the bathroom. He took her by the shoulders and turned her into his broad chest, stroking the back of her head and making gentle soothing noises that totally disarmed her.

'Shh, *mio piccolo*. I didn't mean to upset you. There now...'

Isla breathed in the citrus and spice scent of him, her face pressed against the steady thumping of his heart. His other arm was around her waist, holding her as securely as an iron band. 'Sorry about this...' Her voice was muffled by her face buried in the front of his shirt.

'Don't apologise. I'm the one at fault.'

Isla eased back a little and sniffed, not quite able to meet his gaze. 'It's hormones—it must be. I...I never cry normally.'

Rafe reached behind her to pluck a tissue out of the box on the marble counter and, lifting her chin with his finger, gently mopped beneath her stream-ing eyes, his expression so warm with concern it made her want to cry all over again. 'A lot has hap-pened in a short time. Your life has been completely overturned. And I hold myself entirely responsible for it. Forgive me for upsetting you, *tesoro*. It was not my intention.'

He handed her another tissue and Isla blew her nose and, easing out of his hold, turned to look at her reddened complexion in the mirror. 'Argh. That's why I never cry. What a mess.'

Rafe met her gaze in the mirror and smiled and stroked his hand down from the back of her neck to the base of her spine. 'Personally, I don't think you've ever looked more beautiful.'

Isla turned from the counter and faced him, some-how her hands ending up resting on the hard plane of his chest. 'Would you mind if I gave dinner a miss? I don't feel like going downstairs tonight...'

He brushed a stray curl away from her face. 'I'll bring you something up on a tray. How does that sound?'

'It sounds perfect.'

CHAPTER SIX

RAFE CAME BACK upstairs with a meal on a tray, after giving his housekeeper the rest of the evening off, but when he entered the bedroom Isla was sound asleep. She was curled up on her side, the red-gold cloud of her hair spread out over the pillow, one hand resting on the swell of her belly, the other lying under her cheek. He was in two minds whether to wake her or not. She needed her rest but she needed food too.

And he needed to keep his hands off her.

But he wanted her with an ache that wouldn't go away. Touching her earlier had stirred his desire into a throbbing beat that barrelled through his body even now. He had called on every bit of willpower he possessed, and then some, to keep his desire in check. He didn't want to be blinded by lust, so blinded he got caught out a second time.

He was determined to take things slowly this time. Slowly but surely, that was his plan.

The future was what he was focused on—their

future as a family. He had to show her she had a place in his life as his wife and partner and mother of their child.

A permanent place.

Rafe placed the tray on the bedside table with as little noise as possible. He sat on the edge of the bed beside her curled-up legs and pressed his hands hard against his thighs to stop himself from touching her.

Let her sleep. Let her sleep. Let her sleep. He chanted the words in his mind but to no avail. He found himself brushing a corkscrew curl away from her face and her periwinkle blue eyes opened and met his.

She gave a self-conscious smile and pushed herself up into a sitting position. 'I must have fallen asleep…' She glanced at the fragrant array of food on the bedside table and a little frown tugged at her forehead. 'Gosh. That seems a lot of food for one person…'

'You're not one person at the moment,' Rafe said, placing the tray across her lap. 'You need to feed the baby that's growing inside you.'

Her gaze shifted but her frown didn't go away and her teeth sank into her lower lip. 'Rafe…'

'Eat first. We can talk later.'

He handed her the cutlery and her gaze slowly crept up to meet his. 'I just wanted to thank you for earlier. You've been so kind and I've been a bit of an ungrateful cow towards you.'

Rafe brushed back another stray strand of hair off her face, tucking it behind the neat creamy shell of her ear. 'This isn't an easy time for either of us. You more than me. But I'm confident we can make this work. We have to. We have a child in common and he or she has to be the priority going forward.'

Isla's frown crept back between her eyebrows and she began to pick at the food. 'Have you ever changed your mind once it's made up?' she asked after a moment.

'Not often.'

She gave him the side eye. 'Were you this stubborn as a child?'

'Always. I drove my mother nuts.'

'I can well believe it.' She picked up a plump juicy strawberry from the fruit plate on the tray and bit into it with her small white teeth.

Rafe wanted to suck the juice off her luscious lips right then and there and had to freeze every muscle in his body to stop from doing it. Desire rippled through him in waves, heating his flesh, hardening him to stone.

'Why are you looking at me like that?' Isla asked, wiping her fingers on the linen napkin.

'How am I looking at you?'

A faint blush crept into her cheeks and she swept her tongue across her lips. 'You know how.'

Rafe picked up a strawberry from the plate and held it close to her mouth. 'I like watching you eat.'

He liked watching her, full stop. She could be watching paint dry and he would still find it fascinating to observe her.

She took a small bite of the strawberry, chewed, swallowed and licked her lips. 'Doesn't it make you hungry?'

He kept his gaze locked on hers. 'Ravenous.'

A glimmer of mischief sparked in her gaze and she took the half-eaten strawberry from his hand and held it against his mouth. 'Why don't you have a bite?'

There was something deeply erotic about placing his lips where hers had been just moments earlier. He bit into the soft flesh and the sweet flavour burst in his mouth. 'Mmm… Delicious.'

She picked up another strawberry but, before she could bring it to his mouth, he took her wrist in a gentle but firm hold. He didn't want strawberries. He wanted her. The strawberry dropped out of her hand with a soft little thump that sounded loud in the silence. The tip of her tongue came out to lick her lips and her pupils flared as his head came down so his mouth could meet hers.

The sweetness of the strawberry had nothing on the sweetness of Isla's mouth. Rafe lost himself in the softness of her lips, the playful dance of her tongue as it met the entry of his. The fire of lust licked along his flesh like tongues of flame, his blood surging south with the force of a nuclear missile. His hands went around her, drawing her closer so he could deepen the kiss even further. The meal tray rattled between them and he released her and lifted his mouth off hers with a muttered curse. He removed the tray from across her lap and set it back on the bedside table.

He came back to take her face in both his hands, desire thrumming through him like rapid drum beats. 'Now, where was I?' he asked with a smile.

Isla placed her hands on his wrists, pulling them down from her face, a shadow passing through her gaze. 'Is this going to be like last time? You holding back just to prove a point?'

Rafe frowned and gathered her hands in his in a gentle hold. Her comment was a timely reminder that he was moving too fast. His willpower had its limits and tempting it beyond its endurance was not such a great idea until their relationship was on more secure footing. 'It's not going to be like last time because we're not doing this until you're wearing my engagement ring. I've organised for us to select one tomorrow.' No way was he introducing her to his *nonna* without a ring on her finger.

Her eyebrows rose. 'Isn't that a little old-fashioned of you all of a sudden? What happened to the man who took me back to his hotel room and got me naked in under an hour?'

Forty-two minutes. And during each one of them Rafe's body had been humming and thrumming with lust. The moment he'd laid eyes on her he'd wanted her. It had never happened that way with another woman before. Sure, he'd had plenty of casual encounters in his time, but he couldn't remember one that had captivated him from the very moment their gazes met. Engaging in conversation with her had only reinforced his determination to have her. And knowing she had felt exactly the same way had made it one of the most exciting encounters of his life. *The* most exciting.

'Patience, *cara*. We have the rest of our lives together.'

Isla pulled her hands out of his hold and folded them across her chest, glowering at him. 'You're so confident I'm going to fall in with your plans. But I have a mind of my own, Rafe. I told you before— I will not be bullied into marriage. Marriage is for people who love each other and want to spend the rest of their lives together.'

Rafe rose from the bed and stuffed his hands in the pockets of his trousers. He figured it was better to put them there than reach for her and show how love was not necessary when it came to the chemistry they shared. 'The romantic love you're talking about is largely a fantasy. It doesn't last. So many supposedly madly-in-love couples end up divorcing after a couple of years together. We have a much better chance of making it work because we're starting with realistic expectations and the right motivation to do the best thing for our child.'

'What has made you so cynical about love? Did some woman in your past break your heart?'

Rafe gave a short laugh at the thought of himself falling in love. He hadn't even come close. He hadn't allowed himself to. Loving someone blinded you and left you vulnerable. He had loved his father and look how that had turned out. The father he had loved and modelled himself on had been nothing but a lying, cheating fraud. There was no way he ever wanted to feel that level of disappointment and devastation again. 'No. I've never been in love. I've just seen what being in love looks like and what it does to people when it ends.'

Isla uncrossed her arms and rested her hands on the swell of her belly, a frown still etched on her forehead. 'But surely for a percentage of people it doesn't end. It lasts for a lifetime.'

'Maybe, but there are no guarantees.' He took his hands out of his pockets and moved to collect the tray from the bedside table. 'Are you done with this?'

'Yes. I've had enough.'

Rafe picked up the tray and turned to look at her again. 'I don't want you to think I'm completely without feeling, Isla. I care about you and the baby. You do know that, *sì*?'

Her eyes flicked away from his. 'I'm not asking you to fall in love with me.'

'Are you not?'

Her gaze met his but it was as if there was a screen

up. 'Men like you don't fall in love with women like me. Not outside fairy tales, that is.'

'Now who's sounding cynical?' Rafe said, softening it with a smile. 'Is there anything else I can get you? Another juice or tea or—'

'I'm fine. Please don't fuss. I'm not ill—just pregnant.' Her tone had an edge of irritation that made him wonder if it was masking hurt. But he didn't feel comfortable making promises he couldn't deliver on. Love was a no-go zone for him and he had good reasons for it. It was an emotion he didn't trust.

Could never trust again.

Once Rafe left the bedroom Isla lay back against the pillows with a heavy sigh. She wasn't sure why she kept pushing him on the subject of love. It would be a disaster if she fell in love with him. An unmitigated disaster, because her background would make it all but impossible for him to love her back. Rafe was a proud and intensely private man. The disclosure of her lurid past would destroy any hope of a future together. How could anyone in their right mind, herself included, think she was good enough for someone like Rafe? Like him, she had never fallen in love before, but a secret part of her dreamed of doing so. To be in a relationship with her partner, who openly expressed the same love she felt for him.

But how could she allow herself to hope Rafe would be that partner?

But the more he talked about marriage and bringing up their baby together, the more tempting it became. She didn't relish being a single parent. Her mother had struggled to cope with the demands of a small child, especially once Isla's father had left. Their marriage had only come about because of her mother's pregnancy with her and it had been a mistake from the get-go. Her father had been an immature man-child himself, no way ready to take on the responsibilities of parenthood. When the marriage folded, Isla's mother had dropped into a cycle of self-medication with prescription drugs and alcohol. Isla had far too many distressing memories of gnawing hunger while her mother slept off yet another hangover. Shivering with cold when there wasn't enough money to pay the heating bills. Shouts and slaps and sarcastic put-downs when her mother had run out of her drug or drink of choice, blaming Isla for the train wreck of her life. Then, after her mother's death and her father's subsequent rejection, Isla had spent her childhood being passed around foster homes, never belonging, never fitting in, never feeling loved.

A marriage between her and Rafe might not have any of the financial hardship of her parents' marriage but it would still be a duty-bound contract, not a love-bound one.

Could she risk it for the sake of their child?

* * *

The following day Rafe took Isla to a jewellery designer he knew in Palermo, where the designer escorted them to a private room and brought out an array of exquisite rings for her inspection. Isla knew she should have put her foot down earlier that morning about Rafe's insistence on buying a ring but somehow found herself going along with his plans. Perhaps wearing his ring would stop his housekeeper from eyeing her with undisguised distaste. Besides, they were due to visit his grandmother that afternoon and she knew it would be easier to meet the old lady wearing Rafe's ring than without.

The designer left them alone with a selection of rings and Isla's gaze homed in on a simple mosaic setting, the tiny individual facets glittering brilliantly as each caught the light. It wasn't the biggest ring in the selection and it was set along more traditional lines but she loved it on sight.

'May I have this one?' Isla pointed to it.

'This one?' Rafe lifted it out of its velvet home and took her left hand. 'Let's see if it fits.' It slid over her finger as if it had been made specially for her. He smiled. 'It suits you.'

Isla tilted her hand this way and that to watch the diamonds glinting. 'It's beautiful…' She glanced up at him and added, 'I hope it's not too frightfully expensive. There aren't any price tags and—'

'It's not a problem.'

Isla immediately felt gauche for mentioning price tags. Of course, Rafe didn't have to worry about price tags. He could afford any ring in the store—*every* ring when it came to that. She waited to one side while he paid for the ring on his credit card and then, once he was done, he came to take her hand and led her out of the shop.

'Thank you,' Isla said. 'It's a gorgeous ring.'

'I've ordered a wedding ring to match. Pablo is going to work on it straight away.'

It was on the tip of her tongue to tell him not to bother ordering a wedding ring but something stopped her. Would it be a mistake to marry him? He was the father of her child and would love and provide for it and not shirk parental responsibility like her father had done. Marriage to Rafe would offer her and the baby the sort of financial security she could only dream of. Money wasn't everything, and it certainly wasn't the best motivation for marrying someone, but to never have to worry about providing for her child was a big inducement, one she found increasingly hard to resist.

'I'm thinking a small wedding with just close friends and immediate family,' Rafe said on the way back to the car. 'I have a dress designer in mind but if you have someone you'd rather use then feel free.'

'I don't have any family to speak of,' Isla said. 'And I would only want Layla and a couple of other friends as bridesmaids.' She waited a beat and added, 'How soon are you thinking?'

He glanced at the swell of her abdomen. 'Two weeks.'

Her eyes rounded to the size of dishes. Satellite dishes. 'Are you crazy? No one can organise a wedding *that* quickly.'

A glint appeared in his hazel gaze. 'Watch me.'

CHAPTER SEVEN

AFTER A LIGHT lunch at a café they had dined in previously, Rafe drove the seventy-odd kilometres to the historic coastal town of Marsala in western Sicily, made famous for its fortified wine and ancient ruins. Isla hadn't visited it when she was involved with Rafe a few months ago but had read about the Stagnone Nature Reserve with its salt pans and migratory birds.

Lucia Bavetta's small but beautiful villa was situated not far from the main square of Marsala. A demure housekeeper in her late sixties called Maria opened the door, exchanged a few words with Rafe, smiled briefly at Isla before leading them inside and then melted away like a shadow. Rafe put his arm around Isla's waist and led her to where the old lady was waiting in grand style in the salon.

The well-preserved old-world furnishings gave the room a time capsule atmosphere that made Isla feel distinctly out of place. There were some concessions to modernity—the old lady was sitting in a recliner chair, surrounded by books and newspapers, a tablet and television remote control and a phone set, giving the impression she spent most of her time residing there. There was a walking frame parked nearby and the room had clear pathways between the furniture for ease of passage. There was an elderly tortoiseshell cat curled up asleep on a nearby sofa. It was so still that at first Isla thought it was a taxidermy model, but then it opened one slitted golden eye, made a croaky *miaow* and then went back to sleep.

Lucia's black button eyes coolly assessed Isla's abdomen even before Rafe could make the introductions. 'So, you have brought your latest mistress to meet me.'

'Isla is not my mistress, Nonna. She is my fiancée.' Rafe's tone was firm, his arm around Isla's waist protective.

The old lady raised her chin, her dentures clacking in disapproval. 'When is the wedding? Sooner rather than later, one would hope.'

'Saturday fortnight,' Rafe said. 'I'd like you to be there.'

Lucia grunted noncommittally and waved an imperious hand towards the sofa opposite her chair. 'Sit. But mind Taddeo there. It's straining my neck looking up at you both.'

Once they had sat side by side on the sofa next to the sleeping cat, the old lady turned her attention to Isla. 'My grandson tells me you're an artist. Are you any good?'

'Erm…I'm not sure I'm the right person to answer that,' Isla said, gently stroking the elderly cat, which set off a round of audible purring.

'She's very good,' Rafe said, holding Isla's hand against his muscle-packed thigh. 'I've asked her to paint your portrait in time for your ninetieth birthday. She would need you to do a few sittings for her.'

Lucia made a self-deprecating noise. 'That's all I do, day in and day out—sit. My legs won't do what I want them to do any more. I fall over even when there's nothing to fall over.'

'It must be very frustrating for you,' Isla said.

Lucia glanced at Taddeo, who had now rolled onto his side so Isla could stroke his belly. Her gaze came back to Isla's. 'How many sittings would you need?'

'Two or three to start with,' Isla said. 'I can take photos to work from as well, but I like spending time with the subject of a portrait. It's when I observe their mannerisms or micro-expressions that define their character.'

The old lady folded her hands in her lap as if she had come to a decision. 'When would you like to start?'

Isla didn't like to say she had already started. From the moment she'd walked in she'd been taking in the details of the old lady's personality. Lucia Bavetta presented as a starchy and critical old-school woman who didn't suffer fools gladly, and yet Isla could see traces of the much softer girl and young woman she had once been before the vicissitudes of life had toughened her up. 'I could take some preliminary photos with my phone today and then make a time to come back for a more formal sitting.'

The old lady's bird-like eyes narrowed. 'Don't you have a wedding to plan?'

'Erm…it's not going to be a big affair—' Isla began.

'I've got it in hand,' Rafe said. 'Working on your portrait will be a nice distraction for Isla. Won't it, *cara*?'

Isla smiled a weak smile. 'A distraction right now would be good.'

They ended up staying longer than Rafe expected but his *nonna* insisted on serving refreshments that her housekeeper and long-time companion, Maria, had prepared. But, given he had a surprise in store for Isla that was being prepared back at the villa while they were out, it suited him to dawdle a little over coffee and cake.

Once they'd said their farewells, Rafe led Isla back out to his car. 'That went well, I thought. She likes you.'

Isla swung her gaze to him in surprise. 'You think so?'

'You liked her cat and it liked you. You're in, as

far as Nonna is concerned. "Love me, love my arthritic flea-bitten cat" is her credo.'

She gave a visible shudder and rubbed her hands up and down her upper arms. 'Does it have fleas?'

He laughed and gently brushed his bent knuckles against her cheek. 'Only teasing. There isn't a flea in the world who'd have the courage to enter Nonna's villa, much less reside on her precious cat's body.'

Isla's smile made something in his chest loosen. 'I like your grandmother. She's a straight shooter but has a softer side she takes great pain to keep hidden.'

A family trait? Rafe brushed the thought aside. He had no problem with showing his softer side when the occasion demanded it but there was no way he was going to allow feelings to cloud his judgement—or at least not again.

Rafe opened the passenger door for her and pulled down the seat belt once she was seated. 'Thank you for being patient with her. That could have gone very badly.'

Once they were on their way, Isla swivelled in her seat to look at him. 'Was your mother like your grandmother? In temperament, I mean.'

Rafe sometimes found it hard to think of his mother without feeling a sharp stab of pain at how her life had turned out. Estranged from her own mother, strung along for years by a man who'd claimed to love her but who wouldn't give up his meal ticket marriage for her, only to die of cancer the year after she had been rejected by the man she loved. 'Not in temperament, no. She was *too* soft. Gave too much of herself to other people—my father in particular.'

'Did your father love her, do you think?'

He gave a bark of cynical laughter. 'My father is incapable of loving anyone but himself.' He sighed and continued, 'My mother wanted a different life but didn't have the courage to fight for it. She went along with my father's empty promises for years, hoping he would one day leave his dead marriage and formalise their relationship.' His fingers tightened on the steering wheel. 'She did it for me. Like most mothers, she wanted the best for me even if it meant sacrifice on her part. But she didn't live long enough to see her wishes fulfilled.' He forcibly relaxed his grip and added, 'Nor will she get to meet her grandchild.' He glanced at Isla but she was chewing her lip as if deep in thought. Or deep in worry. Was she comparing his mother's situation with their current one? Seeing similarities that were not really there?

He reached for her hand and placed it on his thigh. 'Stop worrying, I am not like my father. I've made a promise to you and our child. I won't break it.'

She gave a fleeting movement of her lips that almost passed as a smile. 'What was her name?'

'Gabriella.'

'If we have a girl we could name her after your mother if you like.'

Rafe glanced at her again, his heart suddenly feeling as if it had slipped from its moorings. Her gaze was warm and soft with compassion and he realised with a jolt that his mother would have adored her. His mother would have admired her for her strength and courage, for her ability to speak her mind. 'You wouldn't mind?'

Her smile was like a flash of sunshine on a cloudy day. 'Of course not. It's a gorgeous name—although we might have a boy.' Her smile dimmed and she removed her hand from his thigh. 'I don't suppose you want to name him after your father?'

Rafe gave her the side eye. 'No.'

There was a silence, broken only by the sound of the car tyres passing over the road.

He glanced at Isla. 'Your mother won't get to meet her grandchild either.'

She looked down at her hands, where her fingers were fiddling with her engagement ring. 'No, but that's probably a good thing. She wasn't a born nurturer. If she hadn't got pregnant with me, I don't think she would have ever had kids.'

Rafe hated to think of what Isla must have endured as a child for her to end up in long-term foster care. She deserved so much better. *So* much better. And he would do everything in his power to make sure she got it to make up for all she had missed out on. Her revelations about her background made him realise what an amazing strength and resilience she had. No wonder he had felt so drawn to her from the moment they'd met. His background was no way as difficult as hers but it had left its mark. 'I have no doubt you'll be a wonderful mother in spite of not having a good role model. Besides, you will have me to support you every step of the way.'

Her gaze met his briefly before flicking away again. 'My father once told me my mother trapped him by deliberately getting pregnant.' Her voice was toneless, stripped bare of emotion, and yet he could feel it throbbing just beneath the surface. 'He married her out of a sense of duty and because of family pressure, but he never loved her or me, when it came to that.'

Rafe reached for her hand and brought it to his chest, laying it against his heart. No wonder she was baulking at his proposal. But he would make sure she had every reason to feel secure. 'No one is pressuring me to marry you, Isla. I want you to be my wife and I want us to bring up our child together. Deep down, I think you want it too. Over time, the love we have for our child will only strengthen the bond between us.'

There was another small silence.

'I'm sorry I didn't tell you straight away about the pregnancy,' Isla said. 'In hindsight, it looks so selfish of me but I really thought I was doing the right thing under the circumstances.'

Rafe gave her hand a gentle squeeze and brought it up to his lips, pressing a kiss to her bent knuckles. 'You have to learn to trust me, *tesoro mio*. Now, I have a surprise for you. It will be waiting for you when we get home.'

Home. Isla wondered if she would ever look upon Rafe's villa as her home, especially with his guard dog housekeeper Concetta on site. But when they returned to the villa there was no sign of the housekeeper.

Rafe took Isla's hand and led her to one of the downstairs rooms overlooking the garden and water feature. He opened the door and waved his hand for her to precede him. She stepped inside the room and gasped when she saw the array of art materials, including an easel, worktable and drop sheet covering the parquet flooring. He had even had a small sink installed so she could wash her brushes without leaving the room. 'Oh, Rafe, it's amazing. How on earth did you do all this?' She swung around to look at him. 'Thank you so much.'

He smiled. 'I thought it best to give you a room downstairs, given your pregnancy. I don't want you climbing up and down those stairs too much. If I've forgotten anything or you need any other supplies, write me a list and I'll get them for you.'

Isla picked up one of the top-notch brushes and ran her fingers through the soft bristles. He was assuming she would be here right to the end of her pregnancy and beyond. She wanted to be angry with him for railroading her into formalising their relationship, but how could she feel anything but grateful for the way he was handling the situation? She realised she *wanted* to stay with him. To be married to him and provide a safe haven for their child, even if it meant she was a little short-changed on the thing she wanted most of all—love. She glanced at him. 'Everything's wonderful. I could never afford brushes like this. I can't wait to get started on your grandmother's portrait.' She put the brush down and came over to him. 'I don't know how to thank you.'

He brushed a strand of hair away from her face, his eyes dark and smouldering. 'A kiss will be enough.'

Isla stepped up on tiptoe and, linking her arms around his neck, planted her lips on his. For a moment she thought he wasn't going to respond, but then the heat from his lips seeped into hers and suddenly their mouths were pressing against each other in the hungry drive for deeper contact. Lips parted, tongues partnered, desire leapt and danced like roaring flames.

Rafe's arms went around her and hauled her closer, her pelvis pressed against his growing hardness. The intimate contact sent her senses into a tailspin, the need for his possession so rapid, so sudden, so overwhelming it swept through her like an unstoppable tidal wave.

He groaned at the back of his throat and pressed her harder against his erection, the desperation in his kiss matching hers. Her tongue played with his in little cat and mouse movements that escalated the passion flaring between them.

One of his hands came to her breast, cupping it through her clothes, but it wasn't enough. She wanted skin-on-skin. She ached and burned for his intimate touch. 'Please, Rafe, touch me.' Her voice came out breathless and laced with longing.

He found the zipper at the back of her dress and slid it down until the dress was in a puddle at her feet. Isla stepped out of the circle of fabric, feeling no shame at being in just bra and knickers with her ripening belly on show.

His eyes devoured her shape, his hand caressing the mound of her abdomen in a worshipful fashion. 'You're so beautiful, so curvy and gorgeous I can hardly stand it.' His tone was rough around the edges, his gaze burning with incendiary heat.

'Make love to me.' It was part demand, part plea but she was beyond caring how she came across. Need was gripping her so hard it was close to pain.

He framed her face with his hands, breathing deeply. 'I'm not making love to you on a drop sheet on the floor. We'll finish this upstairs in bed.'

Shame suddenly found Isla like a spotlight homing in on a target. Rafe was still fully dressed and here she was, standing in her underwear like a desperate wanton practically begging him to make love to her. It was yet another reminder of the power imbalance between them. He wanted her but far less than she wanted him. She pulled out of his hold and turned to snatch up her dress off the floor. 'Why do you always *do* that?' Her voice was so sharp it could have sliced through concrete.

Rafe frowned. 'Do what?'

Isla stepped back into her dress and worked the zipper up as far as she could. 'I remember a time when nothing would have stopped you making love to me, no matter where we were.'

He came over to her and reached for her hand but she whipped it out of reach. '*Cara*, what's wrong? Why are you being so tetchy? I'm simply thinking of you.'

She bit her lip and turned her back, annoyed at how close to tears she was. That would be the ultimate humiliation—to end up in floods of tears again. 'I know you don't want me as much as I want you, but you don't have to rub it in every flipping chance you get.'

He came up behind her and placed his hands on the tops of her shoulders, slowly turning her to face him. His expression was still etched in a frown. 'You think I don't *want* you? Why do you think there's been no one since you left?' His voice was rough with an emotion she couldn't name. 'I want you so badly it gnaws at me night and day. Every day since you left it's tortured me.'

Isla swallowed. 'Really?'

His frown faded and he gave a lopsided smile, his hands coming up to cradle each side of her face. 'No one turns me on like you do.' He pressed a kiss to her mouth, once, twice, three times. 'But I'm worried about hurting you or the baby.'

'You won't hurt me, Rafe,' Isla said, winding her arms around his waist. 'It's perfectly fine to have sex when you're pregnant. In fact, the hormones right now are making me crazy for you.' It touched her that he had only been thinking of her and the baby, putting his own desire on hold for her sake and that of their child. It made her feel ashamed for jumping to the conclusion that he didn't want her as much as she wanted him. And the thought of him being celibate all this time made her feel even more special. The magic they had shared had left an impression on him that he hadn't wanted to erase by sleeping with someone else. She didn't have the words to describe how much that meant to her.

The most recent memory of a woman's touch on him was hers and hers alone.

He dropped another kiss on her lips and then he gathered her up in his arms.

'Eek! What are you doing? I'm way too heavy,' Isla protested.

His hazel gaze smouldered with desire. 'I'm taking you upstairs to bed. Any further objections?'

Isla looped her arms around his neck and smiled. 'Not a single one.'

A short time later Rafe lowered Isla until her feet touched the floor of the master bedroom, sliding her body down the hard length of his. Every inch of the journey down his body set her senses on fire. He held her against him, one firm arm around her waist and his other hand gently cupping the side of her face. His eyes were as dark as a forest— earthy brown and leafy green and shadow black, with glints of desire as brilliant as slivers of sunlight. 'Are you sure about this?' A battle played out in his gravel and treacle tone—a battle between desire and concern.

Isla placed her hands on either side of his face, her need for him a pulsing ache between her thighs. Her appreciation of his tenderness about her condition made it all but impossible to remember why she had hated him. How could she hate such a man? A man who made her feel such magical sensations. Who made her feel alive in a way she had never felt before. 'I want this. I want *you*. Now.'

He lowered his head and covered her mouth with his, the movement of his lips slow and drugging at first, but then the intensity changed like a switch had been turned. Heat exploded between their mouths, their tongues colliding in passion, hot streaks of longing firing through her like arrows of flame.

Isla's hands went to the waistband of his trousers, desperate to hold him, to feel the heat and power of him. To feel his blood pounding for *her*. Only for her. But he held her off by walking her back towards the bed, sliding down the zip on her dress, his warm firm hand caressing her naked back in one long, smooth stroke that made every nerve sit up and take notice.

His smouldering gaze threatened to incinerate the wallpaper off the walls, his touch on her body creating an inferno of lust. 'Let's not rush this. I want to savour every moment.' His deep voice was another stroke down the length of her shivering spine. Low and deep and seductive.

'I want to rush. I was ready half an hour ago. Stop torturing me, damn it.' Isla set to work on his shirt, tugging it out of his waistband and doing her best to undo the buttons, which were not cooperating with her haste-driven fingers.

Rafe laid his hand over hers, stilling its frenzied movements. 'That was our mistake in the past. We rushed headlong into an affair and didn't take the time to get to know one another first. I want things to be different now. I want to know you in every sense of the word.'

A tremor of shame rippled through Isla. The portfolio of saucy photos flashed through her mind. He didn't need to know *everything* about her. There were some things that were best left in the shadows. She couldn't allow him to ever find out about her chequered past. Would do everything in her power to prevent it. She found it hard to hold his gaze and looked at his mouth instead. 'Kiss me, Rafe.'

He bumped up her chin with his finger, meshing his gaze with hers. 'I want to make this work. Us, I mean. Our marriage. And it can only work if we work together.'

She traced his mouth with her finger. 'I want it to work too.' Her voice came out whisper-soft. 'More than anything.'

His gaze intensified. 'You won't regret it, *cara mio*. I'll make sure of it.' His mouth came back down and sealed hers in a kiss that reignited the flames of need in her body.

Her arms went around his neck, her lower body pressed against the hardened heat of his, her mouth moving in unison with his. He deepened the kiss with a slow and deliberate glide of his tongue, calling hers into a playful dance that had distinctly erotic overtones. Need pooled hot between her thighs, her legs feeling like the bones had dissolved.

Rafe laid her on the bed in just her knickers and bra and trailed his hands down the length of her legs to remove her shoes, the sound of them thudding one by one to the floor heralding what was to come. His glittering gaze held hers in a sensual lock that made her inner core pulse with longing. He stood at the end of the bed and shrugged off his shirt, kicked off his shoes and tugged off his socks. He stood with the proud bulge of his erection lovingly contoured by his dark briefs.

'Aren't you going to take those off?' Isla's voice was husky.

His eyes roamed over the curves of her breasts, still encased in her bra. 'You go first.'

She sat up and pulled one strap over her shoulder, then the other one in a slow striptease that made his eyes flare with heat. She kept her gaze locked on his while she reached behind her back for the hook fastening, releasing the bra and tossing it to one side, her naked flesh exposed to the feasting of his hungry gaze.

'And the rest.' His voice had a note of commanding authority that made the back of her knees tingle like sand trickling through an hourglass. No one else's voice could have such a potent effect on her. No one else could render her to such a quivering mess of need.

Isla peeled her knickers down her thighs, past her knees and over her ankles, tossing them in the same direction as her bra. Her body in all its lush ripeness was exposed to his gaze but, instead of feeling uncertain or shy, she felt empowered. His child was growing in her womb, a product of the passion they had shared. A passion that was as unstoppable as the rising and setting of the sun. And just as hot.

Rafe stepped out of his briefs and came to her on the bed, his hand resting on the swell of her abdomen, his eyes holding hers. 'You are so damn beautiful. So sexy it takes my breath away.'

Isla placed her hand over his, her own breathing a little chaotic. 'You won't hurt me or the baby, Rafe. I want you inside me. I want to feel you. I've missed you so much.'

'I've missed you too.' He leaned down and spoke the words against her mouth, then joined her on the bed, drawing her into the circle of his arms.

Isla caressed the hard length of him, moving her fingers up and down his shaft in the way she knew he loved. The agony and the ecstasy were played out on his darkly handsome features—little flinches of muscles and flutters of eyelids a sign of his enjoyment at her touch. He smothered a groan and covered her mouth with his, the meeting of their tongues sending an arrow of need straight to her core.

He moved from her mouth down her neck, taking his time over each delicate scaffold of her clavicles, his tongue leaving a trail of fire in its wake. He moved closer and closer to her breasts, his slow pace both pleasure and torture. Then finally, *finally* his mouth came to her breasts and subjected them to a sizzling caress of teasing lips and gently tugging teeth. Her nipples peaked to tight buds, her sensitive flesh relishing the stroking glide of his tongue. He left her breasts to work down her body, over the mound of her belly and down the other side to the heart of her.

Isla placed a hand on his shoulder. 'Wait. I want you inside me. Please, Rafe, don't make me beg.'

He gave her a look so hot it made the base of her spine tingle. 'I want you too. You have no idea how much.'

She reached for him again, stroking the silk and steel of his body. 'I think I do.' Touching him stirred her own need into overdrive. Every throb and pulse of his blood found an echo in her own body. An erotic drum beat that was as old as time.

He made a growling sound of pleasure and settled between her thighs, adjusting his limbs to make sure she wasn't taking too much of his weight. 'Tell me if I'm going too fast or too deep or—oh, *Dio*...' His words were cut off by another deep guttural groan as she lifted her pelvis to welcome him. His body entered hers in a silken thrust that sent Isla into a spiral of delight, her body wrapping around him as tight as the grab of a fist.

She wouldn't let him slow his pace. She arched up to meet each downward movement of his body, gripping him by the buttocks to hold him to where she needed him most. The need for release was screaming through her sensitised flesh, a need so urgent, so intense it overtook every rational thought. She was

almost to the edge of oblivion, so desperately, ago-
nisingly close, her breath coming in gasps, her body
straining for that final blessed friction. *So close. So
close. So close.* It was a chant in her head in time
with the throbbing need in her body.

Rafe slipped a hand between their bodies, caressing the swollen heart of her, and finally she flew
off into the stratosphere. Waves of pleasure rolled
through her, leaving her spinning in a whirlpool of
sensation that emptied her mind of everything but a
total sense of bliss.

Within moments of her release, Rafe followed
with his own and Isla held him through each shuddering second, delighting in the knowledge she had
evoked such ecstasy for him. That was what had
marked their fling from the moment it started. Making love with Rafe was a mutually satisfying experience that seemed to get better and better the longer
they'd stayed together.

Rafe propped himself up on one elbow, his other
hand idly stroking the curve of her hip. 'For the past
three months I wondered if I'd imagined how good
we were together.'

Isla tiptoed her fingers up and down his sternum.
'I'm glad there's been no one else.'

He captured her hand and brought it up to his
lips, his eyes dark and lustrous with erotic promise. 'Me too.'

CHAPTER EIGHT

ISLA WOKE FROM a deep sleep an hour or so later to find the bed empty beside her. She decided not to be disappointed Rafe hadn't stayed with her. He was a busy man with a global empire to run. She couldn't expect him to put his career on hold for days or months on end for her. Besides, once they were married, they would have to establish some sort of routine to live together harmoniously. His reason for marrying her might not tick all the romantic fantasy boxes but since when had she bought into the happy ever after fairy tale? Nothing about her life so far had any hint of fairy tale about it.

Life had been one long struggle to survive against the odds.

Isla laid her hand on the swell of her belly, feeling the tiny movements of little feet and elbows inside her womb. At least her baby would not have to face the same relentless struggles. Her baby would be protected from neglect and lack of nurture. It would be surrounded by love from both its parents.

And, no matter what happened between her and Rafe, she knew he would always do the right thing for their child. Always.

Isla had a shower and coiled her still damp hair into a makeshift knot on top of her head. Her hand went to her make-up kit but then she decided against it. Rafe hadn't mentioned going out and the only person she would possibly encounter apart from him was Concetta. She knew there would be no pleasing Rafe's housekeeper unless she packed her bags and left.

Isla made her way downstairs to the studio Rafe had set up for her. She sat at the workstation and began some preliminary sketches of his grandmother, now and again referring to the photos on her phone. She lost track of time until her lower back started to protest. She got up from the table, placed both hands at the base of her spine and stretched backwards.

The door opened and Concetta stood there with a tray carrying a pot of tea and a slice of cake. 'The *signor* told me to bring this to you.' Her tone dripped with resentment, her black button eyes hard.

'Thank you, Concetta. That was kind of you.' Isla cleared some space on the worktable and summoned up a smile. 'Did you make the cake yourself?'

'But of course.' The housekeeper placed the tray on the table with a thud and a little clatter of the crockery. 'No packaged food is served in this house.'

Isla could feel the older woman's disapproval like a chilly fog that had entered the room with her. 'For some people, packaged food is a luxury. Or at least it was for me, growing up.' She didn't know why she had revealed that little snippet of information about herself or why she added, 'And sometimes there wasn't even that.' But maybe it was because she suspected Concetta had always seen through her to the scared and lonely child she had once been. Which was why Isla hadn't tried to make more of an effort to get on with her. The housekeeper saw too much. Sensed too much. Knew too much.

The housekeeper's stiff posture softened—her shoulders going down a notch, her tight mouth relaxing slightly. She glanced at the sketches. 'So, you have met the *signor*'s grandmother.'

'Yes, I like her. She's feisty and opinionated but I felt drawn to her in spite of that.' Isla wished she could say the same for Concetta.

Concetta picked up one of the sketches and examined it for a moment. Something passed over her weathered features—tiny flickering shadows as if a painful memory had been triggered. She put the sketch back down and met Isla's gaze. 'If I give you a photograph of someone, can you draw a portrait for me?' There was a different quality to the housekeeper's voice—a softer, more hesitant quality.

'Of course. But it would be great if the person could sit for me for an hour or—'

'Not possible.' The housekeeper's tone was sharp enough to sever steel.

Isla blinked. 'Okay. The photo will have to do then.'

Concetta worked her jaw a couple of times, as if searching for the right words to use. '*Grazie, signorina.* I will bring it tomorrow.' She turned and walked out without another word, closing the studio door with a resounding click.

Isla sighed and, turning back to the tray set in front of her, poured the tea into the cup and took a refreshing sip. It was too soon to tell if the housekeeper was softening in her icy stance towards her, but not too soon to hope.

Rafe had been fighting with himself to give Isla some space in her studio. He'd had to tear himself away earlier before he was tempted to spend the rest of the day in bed with her. But his own work had lost its appeal and all he wanted to do was be with her, getting to know her better, peeling back the intriguing layers of her personality. For a hard-nosed workaholic, the change in his motivation was as surprising as it was a little disconcerting. He realised he felt happy for the first time in years. He realised he was starting to relax. He could even feel less tension in his neck and shoulders.

Yes, *relax*—that word he had erased from his vocabulary.

Rafe found Isla working in thē studio. The remains of the afternoon tea he had instructed his housekeeper to take to her were sitting to one side. Isla's head was bent over a sketch, the quick-fire movements of her pencil across the sketchpad never failing to impress him. She glanced up as he came in and smiled and something in his stomach toppled over. Would he ever get blasé about her smile and the light in her eyes? Her skin was make-up-free, her curly hair half up and half down in a red-gold cloud about her head. She was wearing dove-grey leggings and an oversized white shirt that skimmed her curves in all the right places. His groin twitched as the memory of her touch rippled through him. He only had to be in the same room as her and it caused a storm in his flesh.

'You look hard at work.' He came over to inspect what she was doing but it wasn't a sketch of his grandmother she was working on but one of him. She had drawn him sleeping, covered at the waist by a sheet that clung to his contours like a drape across a marble statue. He had never seen himself asleep before and it felt strange that she had captured that period of vulnerability. 'It's a good likeness.'

Isla placed another piece of sketch paper over it, her cheeks a faint shade of pink. 'It's just a flash sketch from memory.'

He stood behind her, lifted some of her fragrant hair off the back of her neck and planted a soft kiss to her skin. 'I have a charity dinner to attend in Paris next week. I've been invited to chair one of my favourite children's charities. It's a huge honour and I'd like you to be with me—it will be an excellent way to introduce you in public as my wife-to-be.'

Her body visibly tensed under the gentle press of his hands resting on her shoulders. 'I…I thought we were staying here until…until the wedding?'

He turned her around on the swivelling chair to face him. Her periwinkle blue eyes were troubled, her teeth sinking into the softness of her bottom lip. 'You've attended public dinners with me in the past. What's the problem with doing so now? Especially as you're wearing my ring.'

She glanced down at the glittering diamond ring on her left hand, before coming back to meet his gaze. 'No one knew who I was before. I was just one of your casual lovers.' A shadow passed through her eyes. 'I'm not sure I can handle the press attention. It's…daunting.'

Rafe gently squeezed her shoulders. 'It is daunting but I'll be with you. I'll do everything in my power to protect you. You know that, surely?'

Isla slipped off the chair and from under his hold, moving behind the worktable as if in need of a barricade. Her arms were tight around her body, her eyes flicking out of reach of his. 'Why don't you go alone? I can stay here and work on your grandmother's portrait as well as rest.'

Rafe wondered what was causing her to react so

negatively to a trip abroad. 'Isn't Paris one of your favourite places in the world? What's the sudden aversion to going there with me?'

She sucked in a breath, unfolded her arms and steepled her fingers over her nose and mouth. She closed her eyes in a wincing movement, then lowered her hands from her face to glance at him, the colour in her cheeks darkening to crimson. 'Rafe... there's something I need to tell you. I...I was hoping I wouldn't have to but—'

Rafe's stomach pitched. 'What?' His guts roiled with the possibilities. The horrendous unthinkable possibilities. Another man in the background? Was she already married? His chest was suddenly so tight he couldn't take a breath. *Mio Dio, don't let her be already married to someone else.*

She bit her lip again. 'A long time ago...I made a stupid error of judgement. I was desperate for employment and agreed to work in a...in a—' she swallowed and did that little wincing eye movement again '...a gentlemen's club.'

Rafe's scalp prickled. There were clubs and there were clubs. Some were waiting list exclusive. Some were sleazy. Had someone abused her? Hurt her? Sexually harassed her or worse? The thought of anyone touching her inappropriately sent a wave of fury through his body. '*Cara*, if anyone hurt or threatened you in any way then there are avenues to press charges. I can help you seek justice and—'

Isla bent her head to her chest and sighed, her hands gripping the edge of the worktable. 'I was a lingerie waitress, Rafe. I served businessmen drinks in my underwear.' Her tone was as flat and listless as if she were confessing to an unconscionable crime.

Rafe came over to her and took her stiff little hands in his, stroking the backs of them with his thumbs. 'Look at me, Isla. It's in the past. Lots of people loathe their first job. Not everyone has the luxury of choosing a job that looks good on their CV.'

Her gaze slowly crept up to his, shadows of worry still swimming in their blue depths. 'You don't understand... I agreed to have photos taken.' She gave a gulping swallow and continued. 'A port-folio of photos, some of them topless. I don't know why I agreed to it. I was naïve and too frightened I might not keep the job if I didn't do what the boss said. I was in arrears with my rent, I hadn't eaten for three days, and I was so worried I just did what he said. I've regretted it ever since.'

Rafe wasn't one to resort to violence, but right then he wanted to find the man and rearrange his face so that even the world's best reconstructive fa-cial maxillary surgeon would throw their hands up in defeat. He wanted to find those photos and tear them up and force feed them down the sleazy creep's throat. He wanted justice. He wanted Isla to feel safe. He wanted to protect her so she never had to worry again. Ever. It reminded him of his father's scandal and the impact it had on him as a young teenager. The shame that clung to him like sticky mud. It had taken a lot of strength and willpower and growing a thick skin to move beyond it.

Rafe pulled Isla against his chest and stroked the back of her silky head. 'I'm disgusted with that man for exploiting you. Disgusted and appalled. But I won't allow you to run yourself down because of the sleazy actions of some lowlife creep.' He held her away from him to meet her gaze. 'Where are the photos now? Does he still have them? Has he black-mailed you or made any threats to—'

'No, nothing overt but he hinted at it when I left the job after he came on to me.' Her expression was a landscape of pain, regret and lingering shame. 'He wouldn't have deleted them. And they'll never go away if he puts them online.' Fear and defeated resignation coloured her voice.

Rafe's insides twisted into knots that felt as big as tree stumps. 'I want to fix this for you. I *will* fix this for you.' His hands tightened on hers in determination.

'You can't fix this, Rafe.' Tears welled in her eyes and her voice caught and she pulled out of his hold, putting distance between them again. 'You can't fix me. I'm a liability. I have a target on my back and as soon as you announce you're going to marry me, I know what will happen. Those photos will be on every platform, bringing shame and humiliation to me but also to you.'

An ice-cold trickle of realisation went through his mind. 'Is that why you left me the way you did three months ago? Because of *this*?'

Regret and pride flickered across her expression and through her eyes. 'I panicked when I suspected I was pregnant. You were negotiating that huge deal in New York. I knew how important it was to you and I didn't want to be responsible for jeopardising it. You'd told me a little about Bruno Romano, how conservative he was. I thought it was best if I just disappeared out of your life. Easier for you. Easier for me. But then you found me in that Edinburgh hotel and here we are.'

Rafe speared his fingers through his hair with a hand that was visibly shaking. Emotions he had no name for, no time for, rose in him like a foaming, boiling liquid. He didn't know whether to be angry at himself, or sad for her that she had felt she had to keep the knowledge of the pregnancy to herself. That she had trusted him so little. That somehow his career-driven focus had made it impossible for her to tell him.

That *he* had caused her to run away.

He went to her and gathered her close, hugging her, reassuring her with soothing strokes of his hand on her slim back and murmurings of comfort while he tried to get his emotions in order. If he hadn't run into her at that hotel in Scotland, he might never have known about his child. His gut tightened with an invisible fist. He might never have known his own flesh and blood. And the child would have known nothing of him. It was painful to accept he was partly, if not fully, responsible for her decision to keep quiet.

He had set the rules for their fling.

He had insisted on short-term.

He had made her no promises of a future with him.

He had held her close physically but at arm's length emotionally. He had cordoned off his feelings because he never wanted to give someone the power to hurt him, and yet he had hurt her and himself in the process.

And even more distressing—potentially hurt their child.

Rafe eased her back from him to mesh his gaze with hers. 'I don't know how to make it up to you. It pains me to think you felt you had no other choice but to leave the way you did. But we can put that behind us now. We have to put it behind us and move forward.'

She gave him a world-weary smile tinged with sadness. 'You're being very generous about this. But if I had told you at the time, do you think you would have been as understanding?'

Rafe's conscience was having a tug-of-war. He

liked to think he would have been generous and accepting but how could he be so sure? He might have created even more harm by refusing to believe the baby was his or by insisting on a paternity test on the spot, offering her a conditional relationship on the result. Guilt crept over him like a dark accusing shadow, colouring, questioning everything he had once believed about himself. He hoped he was better than that imagined version of himself.

Hoped, but suspected he wasn't.

'Thing is…I'm not sure.' Somehow, he got his voice past the tightness in his throat. 'One thing I do know for sure—I would not have turned my back on my own flesh and blood.'

'Once you'd established it *was* your flesh and blood, which you still haven't insisted upon doing. Why?'

Rafe released her and stepped away, dragging his hand down his face. 'Is that what you want me to do? Insist on black and white proof?'

Something flickered in her gaze. 'I just thought most men would insist on knowing one way or the other, given we were only having a fling.'

'I like to think I'm not most men,' Rafe said with a little grunt. 'I insisted on us being exclusive and I had no reason to believe you betrayed my trust. I still have no reason to believe it.'

Her bottom lip quivered and tears shone in her eyes. 'Thank you.'

Rafe held out his hands. 'Come here.' She stepped forward and placed her hands in his and he pulled her back into the circle of his arms, resting his chin on the top of her head. He breathed in the flowery scent of her, wondering if he would ever walk by a vine of jasmine again without thinking of her. He had to make their relationship work. He had to make up for his mistakes and mishandling of the situation. He couldn't guarantee the press wouldn't have a shame-fest if those photos ever surfaced but he would do everything in his power to prevent it.

Everything.

CHAPTER NINE

A FEW DAYS later Isla was still trying to get her head around the fact that Rafe now knew her scandalous secret. But she had felt compelled to bring it out in the open when he'd mentioned the charity dinner in Paris. She'd figured it was far better for him to be prepared for the fallout if there was one than to be caught off-guard. It had been a risk telling him, yet he had surprised her by showing amazing compassion and comfort. And since she had disclosed her secret he had been particularly tender and attentive towards her.

But, with the wedding date looming, it was still hard for Isla to be totally confident she was doing the right thing by marrying him. Even as she was fitted for a wedding dress with an exclusive Italian designer, a ghost hand of doubt tapped her on the shoulder. *He doesn't love you.* It was impossible to escape from that one tripwire in their relationship. She could wear the most beautiful wedding dress, have the most wonderful ceremony and honeymoon, and yet, without the assurance of those three little words, what did she really have?

A marriage founded on duty, not love.

A marriage between two people who could never be equals.

Isla went to the kitchen in search of a cool drink, where she encountered Concetta preparing the evening meal. The housekeeper had maintained her distance since their conversation in the studio, and Isla wondered if she had changed her mind about bringing her a photo for her to work from.

'Can I help you with anything?' Isla said to test the waters. 'I'm not much of a cook but I can set the table or arrange some flowers.'

Concetta wiped her hands on her apron, her expression guarded. 'Signor Angeliri pays me to cook. I do not need help doing my job.'

Isla perched on one of the stools next to the large centre island, deciding for once not to be daunted by the housekeeper's attitude. 'Weren't you going to bring me a photo to work from? Or have you changed your mind?'

Concetta picked up a carrot and began scraping the skin off in swift movements. 'You have the wedding to see to first. It can wait.' She picked up another carrot and stripped it as well.

'Who's the photo of?'

The housekeeper's hands stilled for a brief moment, the muscles around her mouth tightening. 'My daughter.' Her voice lost its sharp edge and her gaze softened.

'Oh, lovely. What's her name?'

Concetta blinked a couple of times and swallowed. 'Her name was Marietta.'

Was? A prickle of alarm crept across Isla's scalp like the march of tiny ants. Could the housekeeper's choice of word simply be a language issue? English was not her native tongue and it was all too easy to misuse words. Or could it mean her daughter was no longer alive? 'I'm sorry if this sounds intrusive but did you mean—' Isla began.

'She is dead.' The words were delivered in a toneless voice that belied the host of emotions flickering across the older woman's face.

'Oh, Concetta… I'm so terribly sorry. I can only imagine the pain you've gone through—still going through.'

Concetta wiped across her eyes with her forearm and then continued preparing the vegetables. 'It was a long time ago but the pain never goes away.'

'How old was Marietta when she…?'

'Four. She had not even started school.' Her lower lip trembled and she pressed her mouth flat to control it. 'She caught a…a disease. I am not sure how to say in English. Mena…meni…'

'Meningitis?'

'That is the one' She shook her head sadly. 'My husband started to drink after we lost her. It changed him. We were not able to have any other children—I had an emergency hyster…whatever it is in English, after her birth.'

'Hysterectomy?'

'*Sì.*' She sighed and picked up a courgette and sliced off the top and the tail. 'My future died with her. I will never see her married, never hold my own grandchild. There is no end to the pain of losing a child.'

Isla blinked back her own tears and reached across the workbench for the housekeeper's hand, squeezing it in comfort. 'I'm so sorry.' No wonder the older woman was so prickly and unfriendly. She was suffering unimaginable sadness.

Concetta looked down at their joined hands and, after the briefest of pauses, laid her own on top of Isla's. '*Grazie.*' She gave a back-to-business flicker of a smile and moved to the other side of the kitchen where she had laid her purse and keys. She opened the purse and took out a small photograph, brought it back and handed it to Isla.

Isla looked at the image of a dark-haired smiling child and her heart gave a painful spasm. The little girl was wearing a pretty pink dress and had a matching bow in her hair. 'She's gorgeous, Concetta. Absolutely gorgeous.' She glanced at the housekeeper. 'Do you have other copies of this? I don't want to take the only one off you.'

'I have made many copies. It is my favourite picture of her. She was so excited about going to a birthday party.' Concetta's expression was etched with sadness. 'The friend whose party she went to is married now with children of her own.' She gave a wistful sigh. 'But I only have memories.'

'I will enjoy doing her portrait for you. It will be an honour.'

'It can wait until after the wedding. A bride has many things to see to.'

Isla lowered her gaze a fraction. 'Yes, well, Rafe is doing most of the organising. I just have to show up on the day.' She couldn't quite remove the dejection in her tone.

'Do not marry him if you do not love him.'

Isla met the housekeeper's frowning gaze. 'But that's the problem, you see. I *do* love him but he doesn't love me. Not in the way you'd expect a man to love someone they're about to marry.' It was a relief to finally admit how she felt but she wasn't sure if she had chosen the right person to confess it to.

Loving Rafe had crept up on her, or maybe it had been there all the time as her friend Layla had suggested. Now that she recognised the emotion for what it was, she realised it had been there right from the start. As soon as she'd met him she had felt a seismic shift in her body. It had been like two planets colliding and she hadn't been the same since. And not just because of the pregnancy. She had lied to herself, convincing herself she didn't really like him other than sexually. But he was exactly the sort of man she had dreamt of finding—strong, self-sufficient, hard-working, trustworthy and honourable. She knew deep down he was capable of love; she just didn't know if he was capable of loving her. The armour around her heart had been gradually dismantled by each one of his smiles, his touches, his kisses, his compassionate acceptance of her background and the shame of her past.

Concetta wiped her hands on a tea towel. 'Love can grow over time. Do not underestimate him. He is not like his father. He is a good man.'

Isla gave a half-smile. 'I know he is. A wonderful man who has so many amazing qualities.'

But he doesn't love me.

How long could she live on the hope he might one day do so?

Rafe and Isla were having dinner out on the terrace that evening. The weather was perfect for alfresco dining and Concetta had accepted Isla's help in setting up the table with a large scented candle and some flowers from the garden.

Rafe picked up his water glass, having thoughtfully decided to refrain from drinking alcohol during the rest of her pregnancy—a gesture Isla found incredibly touching. 'You seem preoccupied tonight, *cara*. And you haven't eaten much. Are you not feeling well?'

Isla put down the fork she'd been using to shift her food about her plate without getting much to her mouth. 'I was thinking about Concetta.'

He frowned and put his glass back down on the table. 'Has she been difficult again? I'll have a word with her. I know she can be touchy but she hasn't had the easiest life.'

'I know. She told me today about her daughter, Marietta.' Isla's eyes watered up just by saying the wee girl's name. 'She gave me a photo of her so I can do a portrait. Did you know about Marietta? I wish you'd told me earlier. I would have made more of an effort to get on with Concetta. The loss of a child is the worst possible experience.'

His expression was rueful. 'Yes, perhaps I should have told you. But she's a very private person and she doesn't like talking about it. I'm surprised she told you, actually.'

'Yes, well, we didn't get off to the best start but that was probably more my fault than hers,' Isla said. 'I guess I didn't try too hard back then because I knew I was only going to be a temporary fixture in your life.'

He rolled his thumb over the diamond ring on her hand. 'But you're not now.' His gaze was warm, his tone deep and reassuring. But not reassuring enough for her lingering doubts.

Isla turned his hand over and traced her finger down the middle of his palm. 'This charity dinner next week…' She looked up to meet his gaze. 'Aren't you worried about the effect it will have on the people closest to you if those photos were to surface?'

He curled his fingers around hers, his expression grim. 'There aren't too many people particularly close to me so it won't matter what people think.'

'What about your grandmother? Aren't you close to her?'

He released her hand and leaned back in his chair, his features set in intractable lines. 'You have to remember I didn't meet her until I was a teenager. Nonna refused to have anything to do with my mother because she was a married man's mistress. Her lifestyle clashed with Nonna's strict religious beliefs. When my father dumped my mother, Nonna still refused to have any contact with her.'

'It seems stubbornness is a genetic trait in your family.'

He gave a grunt of assent and picked up his water glass and drank a mouthful before placing it back on the table. 'That and pride. My mother discovered she had cancer a few months after my father deserted her. She kept the knowledge to herself, refusing treatment that could have saved her. I think she just gave up because she felt so rejected and ashamed of what her life had become. And because she was too proud to beg to be taken back into the arms of her family.'

Isla frowned in empathy. 'Oh, that's awful, Rafe.

And how terrible for you. You must have felt so alone when she died.'

He gave a crooked movement of his lips that wasn't anything near a smile. 'I made the choice back then to make my own way in life and rely on no one.'

'Is that why you've only ever had short-term relationships?'

Rafe rested one forearm on the table and draped the other arm over the back of his chair—a casual pose that was at odds with the shadows in his eyes. 'It worked back then but I'm ready to settle down now.'

'But only because of my pregnancy. Not because you fell madly in love.' Isla couldn't quite remove the note of despondency in her voice.

His gaze searched hers with an intensity she found distinctly uncomfortable. It was as if he could see *I love you* written across her eyeballs, even though she desperately tried to hide it.

'Isla.' His tone reminded her of a lecturer about to deliver an important message. 'How many gossip magazines have you seen featuring big celebrity weddings? The couples all claim to be madly in love but half, if not most, end in divorce. What happened to the once-in-a-lifetime love they were raving about? Did it die or wasn't it there in the first place?' His mouth twisted in a cynical grimace. 'I tend to believe the latter.'

Isla placed her napkin on the table for something

to do with her hands. 'So...you don't believe there's such a thing as romantic love? Love that lasts for ever. Not for anyone?'

'Maybe for a few lucky people. But you'll usually find one person loves more than the other, and there's your problem right there—almost certain heartbreak.'

'Like your mother?'

He gave a grim nod. 'She gave up everything for my father but he kept her dangling on a string for years and then cut the string. She could have had a different life. A more satisfying and fulfilling one.'

Isla could see why he was so cynical about love but it didn't stop her hoping he might change his mind and experience it for himself with her. Was it too much to ask that he fall in love with her? The woman he was marrying in two weeks, the mother of his child? 'At least she had you,' she said. 'You must have given her much joy and she would be so proud of you now.'

Rafe smiled and pushed back his chair and stood. 'Why don't you go up and prepare for bed? Concetta will clear this when she comes first thing in the morning.'

Isla rose from her chair and began to gather the plates. 'I can do it now. It won't take me long.'

His gaze smouldered with a promise that made her shiver in anticipation. 'I'd much rather you save your energy for what I have planned for you.'

Rafe might not claim to love her but his desire for her was unmistakable. A desire that had been there right from the beginning, from the first moment their eyes had met. It gave Isla hope that out of his desire would come a love that defied the odds, love that blossomed and grew deep and secure roots into their future as a family.

CHAPTER TEN

A FEW MINUTES later Isla turned her back to Rafe in the master suite for him to unzip her dress. He lowered the zip but an inch at a time, planting a soft kiss to each knob of her spine. She shivered in reaction, her need for him already sending her pulse skyrocketing. Her dress slipped from her shoulders and then from around her hips, landing in a pool at her feet. Rafe unhooked her bra and turned her to face him, his eyes feasting on the ripeness of her curves.

'Your body is getting more and more beautiful. I had no idea pregnancy could be so sexy.' His voice was thick with lust, his hands reaching for her breasts, cradling them, touching them with exquisite expertise.

Isla's legs were trembling from the assault on her senses. She felt drunk on his touch, dizzy with longing. She gave a wry smile. 'I might not look so sexy to you in a few weeks' time.'

He cupped her face in his hands and pressed a

firm kiss to her lips. 'You will always be sexy to me. I have never had a more exciting lover. You stir in me desires I didn't even know I had.'

His words created a warm glow through her body. 'I'll let you in on a secret.'

His hands stilled on her hips. 'Another one?'

Isla smiled and wound her arms around his neck, pressing her naked breasts against his chest. 'Not *that* kind of secret. I've never been able to orgasm with a partner before. Only with you.'

He frowned. 'Really? Why didn't you tell me before now?'

She shrugged one shoulder and began to undo the buttons on his shirt. 'Too embarrassed, I guess.'

He placed his hands over her hands working on his buttons, a frown still creasing his forehead. 'You have no need to be embarrassed, *cara*. Ever. Not with me.'

Isla gave a rueful smile and looked at their joined hands. 'I thought I was hopeless at sex but now I realise I didn't have the right chemistry with other people.'

'How many people?' His expression was dark and brooding, as if he was sickened by the thought of her with other men.

Isla raised her brows. 'I hope you're not going to go all double standards on me. You've had plenty of lovers. Why shouldn't I?' Not that she'd had anywhere near 'plenty'. Her number of lovers didn't even go into double figures.

His mouth tightened for a moment and then he let out a breath, his hands going to rest on her hips. 'You're right. I have no right to be jealous.'

Isla gave him a teasing smile. 'You're jealous? You're actually admitting it?'

A dull flush appeared high on his aristocratic cheekbones but his expression was still brooding. 'I hate the thought of other men touching you the way I touch you.' His voice was a deep growl that made her insides quiver.

She pressed a soft kiss to his tight mouth and smiled. 'Stop glowering at me. I've only had two lovers and neither of them were as amazing as you.'

His hands on her hips drew her closer, the ridge of his erection sending a shockwave of need through her entire body. 'What's wrong with those men that they didn't satisfy you? You're the most responsive lover I've ever had.'

She planted another kiss on his lips. 'They weren't you—that's what was wrong.'

He returned the kiss with a low deep groan, his tongue thrusting between her lips to tangle with hers in a sexy duel that sent fireworks fizzing and whizzing in her blood. She felt his sensual excitement running through him, the probe of his aroused flesh and the erotic flickers of his tongue in her mouth making her inner core clench.

Isla continued to undo the buttons on his shirt, leaving a kiss on each part of his chest as she uncovered it. She peeled his shirt away from his shoulders and set to work on the fastening on his trousers. His eyes darkened with desire and he sucked in a breath as her fingers skated teasingly over the hard ridge of his arousal. She lowered herself in front of him, uncovering him so she could tease him with her lips and tongue. His fingers dug into her scalp as if he thought his legs would go from under him without her support. His groans and heavy breathing were a delight to her and she continued her sensual exploration of him, enjoying the power it gave her to reduce him to the same level of longing as he had done to her. *This* was the balance of power she craved—to know he wanted her as much as he wanted his next breath.

He pulled away from her with a desperate groan. 'Stop. I can't take any more. I want to be inside you.'

His words sent a hot, pebbly shiver over her flesh. She took his hand and got to her feet, leading him to the bed, taking off her knickers as she went. Rafe kicked his trousers and shoes to one side and tugged off his socks and came down beside her on the bed.

His mouth went to her breast, kissing, stroking, teasing her nipples into tight and aching peaks. He moved down her body, leaving a blistering trail along her flesh until she was gasping out loud and writhing to get closer, to have him where she most wanted him.

'I want to taste you.' His voice was rough with desire, his warm breath skating over her lower body to claim his prize.

Isla grasped him by the hair. 'No. I want you inside me. Now.'

He gave her a devilish grin. 'Say please.'

'Please, Rafe. Make love to me. Please, please, please.'

'With pleasure.' He came back up to position himself over her, his legs entangled with hers. He drove into her centre with a guttural groan, his movements fast, feverish, frantic. She was with him all the way, welcoming each thrust with a gasp of pleasure. Isla gripped his taut buttocks, holding him to her, desperate for release as the sensations rioted through her body in hot pulsing waves.

With the merest coaxing of his fingers on her swollen centre she was off and flying, her entire body thrashing with a cataclysmic release. Within moments, Rafe followed with his own deep and gravelly groan of desperation, his body shuddering as the ripples of pleasure went through him.

Isla held him against her, stroking her hands over his back and shoulders, delighting in the spray of goosebumps that peppered his flesh. *She* had done this to him. Brought him undone with her touch, with her body—with her love.

How could she call it having sex now? It was making love. Isla had been making love with him from the start. That was why sex had been so awkward with other people. She hadn't been able to give all of herself, to feel comfortable enough to express herself physically. She had needed the connection to be deeper, stronger, more meaningful than just two bodies getting it on.

And what stronger and more meaningful connection could there be other than love?

Rafe propped himself up on one elbow, his other hand idly playing with her hair. 'I thought of you every day after you left.' His voice had a sombre note that matched his thoughtful frown. 'Every single day. And night.' His mouth twisted into a self-deprecating smile. 'I was angry at you but over time I realised I was really angry at myself.'

Isla stroked away the crevasse of his frown between his eyebrows. 'Why?'

He captured her hand and brought it to his mouth and kissed each of her fingertips, his gaze holding hers. 'I hadn't met anyone like you before. Someone who wasn't in awe of my money or what gifts I bought you or places I took you. I liked that about you. It impressed me and, believe me, I'm hard to impress.' His frown came back and he continued, 'I was angry because…it…it *hurt* to lose you.' A flicker of something passed over his face as if saying the word 'hurt' had caused him further pain. 'I hadn't felt like that before. I didn't allow myself to get invested in relationships where it could even be a possibility. I didn't take those sorts of risks.'

Isla gently pulled her hand out of his and sent her fingers on a journey down the length of his richly stubbled jaw. 'But you did with me.' Her voice was barely above a whisper, her hopes barely above water. Was he about to tell her he loved her?

He leaned down and pressed a soft-as-air kiss to her mouth. 'You should come with a warning. Take care when handling.' His tone was mildly teasing, his eyes dark and shining.

Isla circled his mouth with her finger. 'So should you.'

The teasing light went out of his eyes and his frown came back. 'I worry about how much your life has changed because of this—' he placed his hand on the mound of her belly '—our child. You're the one who's had to make the most adjustments so far and that will likely continue.'

She placed her hand over the top of his and tentatively smiled. 'But you'll be with me every step of the way, right?'

His hand came up and cradled one side of her face, his expression grave. 'Never doubt it, *cara mio.*'

Why then was she still doubting? Not that he wouldn't support her during the rest of the pregnancy and beyond. But what about love? What about the special emotion two people felt for each other that would last a lifetime?

The special emotion she felt for him and had done so from the first moment she'd met him.

For ever love.

Isla wondered if she should risk telling him how she felt. But telling someone how she felt had always ended badly when she was a child, so over the years she had taught herself not to reveal and not to feel. Telling the first foster parents how much she loved them had been her first mistake. She had been moved within days to another home, to live with more strangers. Kind strangers who had also over time evoked such feelings of gratitude in Isla that she had told them she loved them too.

And she'd been moved again.

And again.

And again.

Her adult self knew it was the system. Kids didn't always stay long in any one place due to other needy kids needing urgent placements, but as a child it had felt like she was unlovable.

Rafe sent a lazy finger between her eyebrows and down the bridge of her nose. 'What's that frown for, hmm?'

Isla circled her fingers around his wrist, pulling his hand down from her face. 'I need the bathroom... Sorry.' She wasn't ready to tell him. She couldn't tell him and risk being rejected.

Or worse—being reminded she was unlovable.

He rolled aside and got off the bed, holding a hand

out to her, his features etched in lines of concern. 'Are you feeling unwell?'

Isla ignored his hand and pushed herself off the bed, sending a hand through the wild mess of her hair. 'I'm fine, Rafe. I just really need to pee.'

And I need to be alone to get my dangerously tempted-to-confess-all tongue back under control.

The bathroom door closed with a snick of the lock that somehow felt to Rafe like a slap to the face. He scraped a hand through his hair and turned back to look at the rumpled bed. He leaned down and straightened the covers and wished he could just as easily straighten his tangled thoughts. Why had he told her he'd felt hurt when she'd left? *Hurt?* No, hurt was an emotion he never allowed himself to feel. Another word he had deleted from his vocabulary. He made sure he didn't care enough to be hurt by anyone.

But somehow, in the afterglow of good sex, he had revealed things about himself he revealed to no one.

Half the time, not even to himself.

Making love with Isla had a strange effect on him and had done so from the start. In the moments after orgasm, when his body was relaxed and satiated, a guard lowered inside him. The locked vault around his heart developed a small fissure, letting in a tiny sliver of light. It was in that brief window of time he *felt* vulnerable.

There, he had confessed to feeling the dreaded V word.

Vulnerable.

It didn't last long—he didn't allow it to, but the thought of that feeling lurking, waiting for another chance to catch him off-guard, was incredibly disquieting.

A few days later, Isla and Rafe flew to Paris for his charity dinner and he settled her into his penthouse at his hotel in the exclusive and gentrified Saint Germain. He had organised for her to have her hair and beauty treatments done in advance and spent a fortune on a new dress for her that would accommodate her baby bump. The glorious royal blue satin shoulderless dress draped her figure in all the right places, and Isla couldn't help thinking even Cinderella would have been envious.

And yet, now she was in Paris with Rafe, Isla sensed a clock ticking on a time bomb. As soon as the news spread about their impending wedding, as it would surely do after a high-profile event such as this, her private shame had a very real possibility of being exposed to every critical and judging eye. The impact on Rafe and his reputation couldn't be underestimated. Not to mention the impact on her.

Isla sat at the mirror in front of the dressing table in the penthouse, putting the last touches to her make-up, waiting for Rafe to come back to collect

her for the ball. He had been called away to speak
to his hotel manager downstairs but assured her he
would be only a few minutes.

The penthouse door opened and she heard the dis-
tinctive sound of Rafe's footsteps approaching the
bedroom and, when he arrived, met his eyes in the
mirror. 'Everything all right with your manager?'

'*Sì*. All good.' He smiled and took out a flattish
rectangular velvet jewellery box from inside his tux-
edo jacket pocket. 'I have something for you.'

Isla stood from the dressing table stool and gave
him a mock-stern look. 'You didn't really need to
speak to your manager at all, did you?'

His smile became a grin and he handed her the
box. 'I had to ask him to unlock the safe for me.'

Isla took the box from him, flicked the tiny brass
catch open and lifted the lid to reveal a glittering
sapphire and diamond necklace and matching drop-
let earrings. 'Oh, my goodness. They're beyond
beautiful—they're absolutely stunning.'

'Like their new owner.' His voice dropped in pitch
to a deep rough burr that made her spine feel tingly.

Cinderella, eat your heart out. How could Isla feel
anything but beautiful wearing such exquisite jewels? She trailed her index finger over the sparkling
diamonds and densely blue sapphires. 'I'm almost
too afraid to wear them in case I lose them.'

'Don't worry. I insured them three months ago.'

Isla glanced up at him in puzzlement. 'You bought these before? *Before* I...I left?'

Something came down at the back of his gaze with the speed of a camera shutter click. He gave a loose one-shoulder shrug that was at odds with the sudden tightness of his mouth. 'What of it? It's just a gift I bought when I was in New York.'

Just a gift? A pretty expensive gift to Isla's reckoning. To anyone's reckoning. What did it mean? She looked down at the gorgeous jewels and swallowed. 'I don't know what to say...'

'Thank you will be perfectly adequate.' His tone had a sharp edge that brought her gaze back up to his.

'Oh, Rafe...' she said, touching him on the arm. 'It's the most beautiful gift I've ever received. Thank you so much. I'm sorry I wasn't there when you brought it back from New York. No wonder you were so angry with me.'

He let out a long slow breath. 'It wasn't about that.' He took the box from her. 'Here—let me put them on you. Turn around.'

Isla turned her back to him, her skin lifting in a delicate shiver as his fingers touched her skin in the process of fastening the necklace around her neck. The sapphires made her blue eyes pop and she had never felt more beautiful or bewildered. He had bought her gifts before, many gifts that were expensive and gorgeous, but something about this gift was different. She was no jewellery-valuer but this ensemble was clearly worth a fortune.

And he had bought it for her months ago.

Rafe handed her the earrings one at a time, waiting as she inserted them into her earlobes. His hands came to rest on the tops of her shoulders and he smiled. 'They suit you.'

Isla crossed her right arm over her body to place her hand over one of his, meshing her gaze with his. 'Thank you. I will always treasure them, no matter what.'

He bent his head to drop a kiss to the back of her neck. 'We'd better get going, otherwise I'll be tempted to see what you're wearing under that dress.'

Isla laughed. 'Not very much.'

His eyes smouldered with molten heat and he stroked his hand over one of her bottom cheeks. 'That's what I thought.'

CHAPTER ELEVEN

THE BALL WAS being held in a grand hotel on the seventh arrondissement with spectacular views of the Eiffel Tower and the city beyond. Rafe led Isla into the hotel past the throng of the press but the rapid fire of cameras going off was distinctly off-putting. How was she supposed to act calm and poised and comfortable when she didn't belong in Rafe's world?

His world was one of high finance, exotic destinations, glamorous events and even more glamorous people.

Her world was one of salacious secrets and cringe-worthy shame.

A journalist approached and asked, 'Rafael Angeliri, we have heard rumours that the beautiful woman beside you is soon to be your wife. Is that true?'

Rafe's arm gathered Isla close to his side. 'Yes, it is true. We are marrying next weekend in Sicily.'

Isla swallowed and painted a smile on her lips and tried to look as if she was used to having forty cameras aimed in her direction. The journalist glanced at Isla's abdomen and asked, 'We have also heard congratulations are in order for another happy event. Do you have anything to say on that?'

'Isla and I are delighted to be having our first child in December,' Rafe said. 'Now, if you'll excuse us, we have a function to attend.'

Several other journalists vied for Rafe's attention but he led Isla inside the hotel with a firm arm around her. Once they were safely inside and away from most of the crowd of guests waiting to enter the ballroom, he took her hand and kissed the backs of her fingers, holding her gaze with his. 'That wasn't so bad, was it?'

Isla gave a weak smile. 'I seriously think I need to attend press-handling classes.'

He squeezed her hand. 'They're just ordinary people trying to do their job. There will be official photos later but for now try and relax and enjoy the evening.'

And, to her surprise, Isla did enjoy the evening. The food was a stunning example of French cuisine at its best, and the table and ballroom decorations had a Marie Antoinette era look that gave the night a step-back-in-time feel.

Rafe was by her side until he got up to the podium to give his keynote speech. He spoke in fluent French as well as English on the importance of taking care of children in the community. *Every* community. The strategies he proposed for better care of the most vulnerable in the community were well-thought-out and practical, and Isla felt incredibly proud and deeply moved that he was so determined to bring about change.

When he came back to the table after rapturous applause, Rafe leaned down to kiss Isla on the lips before he sat back down. He took one of her hands and rested it on his thigh. 'I'm glad you came with me tonight. It wouldn't have been the same without you.'

'You were wonderful,' Isla said, leaning her head against his shoulder. 'I was so proud of you.'

He turned his head towards her and smiled and something in her stomach swooped. He stroked the curve of her cheek with a lazy finger, his eyes darkening. 'Dance with me?'

'I would love to.'

He drew her to her feet and led her to the dance floor just as the band began to play a romantic ballad. Isla melted into Rafe's arms and moved with him around the floor as if they were one person, not two. Dancing had never felt more graceful, more fluid, more natural than when in Rafe's arms. One song turned into two and then three, and then Isla lost count. She was captivated by the feel of his arms holding her close, the tangy scent of his aftershave teasing her nostrils, the sheer joy of being his entire focus.

Rafe looked down at her with a smile that made her legs weaken at the knees. 'We'll smash the bridal waltz next Saturday now we've had all this practice, *si*?'

A tiny tremor of unease tiptoed through her. *This time next week she would be Rafe's wife.* Was she doing the right thing by marrying him, even though he had never said he loved her? When all was said and done, it was nothing more than a duty marriage. Yes, it was convenient for him that he desired her and enjoyed her company. But he had never claimed to love her and had even intimated he wasn't capable of feeling that way about anyone. Was she being a fool for settling for care and concern and security instead of the love she desired and hungered for?

Isla fought to keep her features in neutral but he must have sensed her disquiet and led her off the dance floor to a quieter area away from the other guests.

'What's wrong, *mio piccolo*?' His tone was full of concern. 'Are you not enjoying yourself?'

Isla smiled her lingering doubts away. She had to stop stressing over what she didn't have and enjoy what she did have. Rafe cared for her. He was prepared to provide for and protect her and their baby. 'I'm having a wonderful time. It's been a fabulous evening. I'm just feeling a little tired now, I guess.'

And in love. Hopelessly, stupidly in love.

He leaned down and gently kissed her forehead. 'Then it is time for me to take my beautiful Cinderella home from the ball.'

Rafe was relieved to leave the ball in any case. He didn't enjoy the spotlight at the best of times, and the last thing he wanted to do was make idle chat with people he didn't know when the only person he wanted to be with was Isla. That was one of the things he'd missed most when she'd left him three months ago. The emptiness at the end of the day when he returned home to his empty villa, when before he had looked forward to their lively debates and verbal tussles that made his blood tick with excitement. Dancing with her made him realise yet again how in tune they were with each other physically. It secretly thrilled him he had been the only lover who had satisfied her. But in some ways the reverse was also true. He had never felt with anyone else the intense level of satisfaction he felt with her.

Once they were back at his hotel penthouse bedroom, Rafe took Isla in his arms and kissed her softly on the mouth. 'You were the belle of the ball tonight.'

She linked her arms around his neck, her eyes as luminous as twin moonlit lakes. 'You don't do too badly in the handsome stakes yourself.' She moved against him, her pelvis setting fire to his. 'But it's time you took off that posh suit.'

Rafe raised a questioning eyebrow. 'Hey—I thought you were tired?'

She pressed herself even closer so he could feel every delicious curve of her body along every hard ridge of his. Her naughty girl smile sent a lightning strike of lust to his groin. 'Not *that* tired.' She stood on tiptoe and planted a series of kisses on his mouth. It was all he could do not to pull up her dress and take her against the wall.

He cupped her bottom in his hands, the smooth satin of her dress sliding against her curves with a sexy swish. 'You should be resting. I kept you on the dance floor way too long.'

Isla whipped off his bow-tie and tossed it to the floor, her eyes sparkling as bright as the diamonds and sapphires around her neck. 'Then you can take me to bed. Now. But you have to undress me first.'

'No problem.' Rafe tugged her dress down to reveal her breasts, the proud and ripe curves with their pregnancy darkened nipples sending every drop of his blood south. He pulled the dress further down and it fell to the floor at her feet, leaving her in nothing but her high heels, her jewels and a tiny lace thong. He cupped her breasts in his hands, feasting on their soft white creaminess against his olive-toned skin. 'You take my breath away every time I look at you.' His voice came out raspy and his need burned like fire in his groin.

She began to unbutton his shirt but she only got

to button number three when Rafe took over the job himself. He hauled the shirt over his head and threw it aside, desperate to feel her hands on him. She was already on to it, her busy little fingers sliding down his zip and finding him. He shuddered at her touch, the play of her hand up and down his shaft driving him crazy with need.

He pulled her hand away, breathing heavily, searching for his self-control but finding it had gone into hiding. 'Let's slow down a bit—'

'Let's not.' Her mouth slammed into his, her tongue snaking between his lips and shooting fire into his mouth and into his blood. His pulse hammered, his heart raced, his lust roared.

One of his hands grasped her by the hip, the other dispensed with the tiny scrap of lace that was barely covering the secret heart of her. He caressed her hot wet centre with his fingers, teasing her into gasping cries of pleasure. He hitched one of her legs up so he could drive into her to experience the contractions of her orgasm around him, triggering his own powerful release. He gave a deep groan and lost himself in the star-exploding storm that shook and shuddered and shimmied through every inch of his body.

Isla ran her hands down his arms with a feather-light touch. 'That's more like the Rafe I know.'

Rafe was still trying to catch his breath. 'What do you mean?'

She circled one of his flat nipples with a teasing

finger. 'Since I've been back, you've been making love to me as if I'm made of glass.' The edge of her mouth came up in a coy half-smile. 'I like it both ways.'

A shiver coursed over Rafe's body. No one could turn him on like her. A sultry glance from beneath those fan-like lashes, a flash of that knock-you-out-cold smile, the sexy scrape of her fingernails along his arm. Everything she did made molten heat flash along the network of his veins, sending his blood pumping, thumping, jumping in excitement.

He took her by the hips again and brought his mouth to just above hers. 'Let's see what I can do about that.'

Isla woke the next morning from a deep and restful sleep to find herself alone in the bed. Nothing unusual in that, for Rafe was an early riser—such an early riser he put most larks to shame. She pushed her hair away from her face and swung her legs over the edge of the bed, smiling when she felt tiny twinges in her inner core. Making love with Rafe had been the perfect way to finish the night of the ball. His compliments had made her glow with pleasure, his touch sending her into raptures time and time again.

She had made a bargain with herself last night to stop fretting about those wretched photos. Her worries about a public exposure of her past might never be realised and it was crazy to put herself under such stress over something she had no control over anyway. Rafe had told her to put it out of her mind—that it was not an issue for him. This time next week they would be man and wife. She had to focus on the future they had, together with their child. A future that might not be as perfect as she had dreamed of, but it would be secure and stable and she, of all people, knew there was a lot to be said for secure and stable.

Isla had a shower and, with her towel still wrapped on her head, came out of the bathroom to see Rafe standing by the bed with a newspaper folded up in his hand. His expression was inscrutable but there was a brooding energy that came off him in waves.

A shiver ran down Isla's spine like a small sticky-footed creature. 'You were up early.' She tried to disguise her worry by leaning to one side and rubbing the towel against her wet hair. 'Did you get some of those gorgeous fresh croissants from the bakery like the last time we were here?'

'Isla.' The note of gravitas in his voice chilled her blood. 'I want you to promise me something.'

She gulped and didn't try disguising it. She couldn't. 'Wh-what?'

'Promise me you won't look at the papers or anything online until this blows over. Okay?'

A cold hand clutched her heart and squeezed, squeezed, squeezed until she could only get enough breath to whisper, 'This?' Her eyes went to the folded newspaper under his arm. 'Oh, God…the photos?' The frozen hand around her heart suddenly let go and the trapped blood gushed and hammered so hard she thought her chest would explode.

A flash of pain went across his face and his eyes looked haunted. 'You have to let me deal with it, *cara*. Trust me. I will deal with it and you will *never* suffer this humiliation again. Understood?' The steely determination in his tone was as reassuring as if he had those dreadful negatives burning to smithereens in front of her right then and there.

If ever there was a man worthier of a white stallion and a suit of armour, Isla would like to see him. Rafe's promise to protect her, to keep her from harm no matter what, was as wonderful as if he had said *I love you*. Didn't that prove how much he cared for her? Why was she worrying about three little words that anyone could say but not always back up with actions?

'You'd do that? For me?' Her voice was just shy of breaking.

He threw the newspaper into the wastepaper bin and came to her and pulled her close against his chest. 'I'm sorry this has happened but we'll ride it out. Don't speak to the press, no matter what. It will only add fuel to the fire.'

Isla looked up at him with tears stinging her eyes. 'I'm so sorry.'

He kissed her forehead. 'You're not the one who should be apologising. I will not rest until I see justice served. You have my word on that.'

It took every ounce of willpower for Isla to walk past that wastepaper bin without pulling the newspaper out. It took willpower to turn her phone's Wi-Fi off so she couldn't look at anything online. It took even more willpower and fortitude to travel to the airport with Rafe and try and ignore the horde of press waiting for them wherever they went. But no amount of willpower could allow her to unhear the salacious questions fired at her like a rapid round of artillery. Each question hit her like a slap. She could feel her face on fire, shame raining down on her, weighing her down so she could barely walk in a straight line, her body hunched against the onslaught.

Rafe kept his arm around her, shepherding her through the knot of paparazzi to the waiting car. 'Don't respond. I'm with you. You have nothing to be ashamed of, *cara*. They are the ones who should be ashamed, not you.'

Rafe was so calm and controlled and yet she sensed he was simmering with an anger so intense she couldn't help pitying the person who'd posted the photos. She had given him all the details she could remember of the man who ran the club and Rafe had already set the legal wheels in motion.

A Sicilian's fierce pride was a potent thing and

it thrilled her that Rafe cared enough about her that he would fight for justice no matter what it cost. For the first time, Isla thought that maybe there was a chance they could ride this out. Rafe was by her side and supporting her. Didn't that count for something? If it didn't matter to him, then why should it matter to her?

Once they were safely in the car, a mantle of peace settled over her. She no longer had to face this alone. He was with her every step of the way.

Rafe reached for her hand and drew it up to his mouth, kissing her bent knuckles. 'Together we will get through this, *mio piccolo*. I won't allow anyone to hurt you. You're safe with me.'

Safe. That was something Isla had never felt before now. 'You have no idea how much that means to me.' Her voice was soft with gratitude, her heart so full with love for him she was surprised he couldn't see it. So what if he didn't love her? She had enough love for both of them.

And maybe in time he would come to love her, as she was sure he would love their child.

They arrived back in Mondello, but they were barely in the door of the villa when Concetta came towards them with a worried look on her face. '*Signor*, you must hurry. Signora Bavetta has just been taken to hospital.'

Isla's heart sank. His *nonna* was ill?

Rafe dropped the bag he was carrying on the floor

with a thud, his features tight with tension. 'Why didn't someone call me before now?'

'The call only just came in from her housekeeper, Maria,' Concetta said. 'They have taken her to the private hospital in Palermo where she went the last time she had a fall.'

'Did she fall again?' Rafe asked, rattling his car keys in impatience.

'No,' Concetta said, glancing briefly at Isla. 'She was reading something on her tablet and she suddenly collapsed.'

Ice-cold dread pooled in Isla's stomach. Had Rafe's grandmother seen the scandal of her past in the press? Was his *nonna*'s illness *her* fault? She looked at Rafe, her hand clutching her chest where her heart was thumping so jerkily she worried she might faint. Her past was never going to go away. It was always going to be a sticking point, if not for Rafe, then for his family and friends and business colleagues.

'Stay here, *cara*,' Rafe said, touching her lightly on the arm. 'You need to rest. I'll call you when I find out how she is.'

Isla grabbed at his wrist, tears already welling in her eyes. 'Why can't I come with you? I want to support you—'

The grim shadow in his eyes was only there for a moment before he blinked it away, but it was there long enough for Isla to know she had no place by his side. Not with him at his grandmother's bedside, given it was *her* scandal that had caused his *nonna* to collapse.

'No, Isla. You must stay here and rest.' His tone brooked no resistance. 'There isn't anything you can do right now.'

Yes, there is. Isla's heart plummeted. *I should have done it well before now.*

CHAPTER TWELVE

ISLA PACKED A few things in an overnight bag and booked an online fare back to London rather than Edinburgh. She needed some time to herself before going back to Scotland to sort out the train wreck of her life. If Rafe found her before she had time to think about her future, she might be tempted to stay with him. But how could she stay, knowing it was *her* mess that had caused his grandmother to become ill?

Her past was not going to go away, no matter how much she wanted it to. No matter how much money Rafe spent on expensive lawyers. No matter how much he tried to reassure her. It was an ugly stain on a white sheet, an indelible stain that spread and spread until now it was tainting others. *Hurting* others. Hurting Rafe—the man she loved more than anyone in the world.

Rafe, whom she loved more than her own happiness.

Isla called a cab and waited in the foyer for it to arrive. Concetta appeared from behind one of the marble pillars with a frown on her weathered features.

'You are leaving? *Again?*' The housekeeper's voice contained a thread of worry. 'But you must not. The *signor* will be—'

'I'm sorry, Concetta, but I must go,' Isla said, fighting to hold her emotions in check. 'Surely you can see that? I don't belong in his life. You've always thought that. Deny it if you like, but we both know I'll only bring more trouble into his life.'

'I admit I didn't like you at first,' Concetta said. 'But that was because I didn't think you were being honest with him. I see now you are good for Signor Angeliri. You make him smile. You make him relax. He doesn't work such long hours when you are here. You cannot just leave him. The wedding is next Saturday.'

'There isn't going to be a wedding,' Isla said. 'I should never have said I would marry him.'

'You make promises and then you don't keep them.' Concetta's black button gaze was scathing. 'It is better not to make a promise in the first place so you don't get people's hopes up.'

Isla steepled her hands around her mouth and nose and let out a deep breath. So, it wasn't only Rafe and his grandmother she had hurt but his housekeeper too. She lowered her hands from her face and met the housekeeper's critical gaze. 'I haven't had much time yet to work on your daughter's portrait. But when it's finished I'll send it to you, I promise. And Rafe's grandmother's portrait too.'

'Pah!' Concetta's tone was as scathing as her gaze. 'If she lives to see it.'

The front door opened and Rafe stepped inside with a frown carved deep between his brows. 'What's going on? Why is there a cab waiting outside?'

'Your *fiancée*—' Concetta spat the word out like a lemon pip '—is leaving.'

Rafe's expression became as unreadable as a MI5 spy. 'Please excuse us, Concetta,' he addressed the housekeeper in a cool and formal tone. 'Isla. The salon. Now.'

He went to take her by the elbow to lead her in the direction of the salon but she stepped out of his reach.

'How is your grandmother? Is she…?' Isla couldn't go any further as dread and shame washed through her in sickening waves.

'She suffered a mild stroke but nothing to worry about. The geriatrician has put her on some blood-thinning medication. She'll be home in a day or two.' His voice remained calm on the surface but there was an undertone of tension. 'But it's you I'm worried about. What's going on? Has Concetta upset you?'

Isla picked up her tote bag from the chair near the hall table and hung it over her shoulder. 'I'm sorry, Rafe, but I have to go. This isn't going to work. I was stupid to think it ever would and I—'

'What's brought this about?' The tension in his voice went up another notch.

'It's me, Rafe,' Isla said. 'Me. You. Us. It can never work. I will only bring shame and disgrace to you and your family.'

He pinched the bridge of his nose—the first sign of a crack in his steely composure. He blew out a breath and locked his gaze on hers. 'I told you I'd handle the photo situation. I've got my people working on it as we speak. You have to trust me to deal with—'

'And what happens in the meantime?' Isla said, her throat tight and throbbing. 'Stand by and watch your grandmother have another stroke when she sees more of those awful photos splashed everywhere? I can't allow that to happen. I can't do it to her or to you.'

A flicker of something passed over his face—a tiny flinch of a muscle near the hinge of his jaw, a blink that lasted a little too long, as if he were mentally closing a blind on a distressing scene. 'Nonna would have had a mini-stroke regardless. The doctor said—'

'So, you're not denying that she saw the photos on her tablet and it caused her to get upset enough to—'

'Isla, it's not your fault.' The heavy chord in his tone told her the opposite. It confirmed everything she believed about herself.

'How can it *not* be my fault?' Isla asked. 'Next it

will be your business taking a hit. Deals being cancelled because of me. The children's charity dumping you as chairman. I won't allow it to happen. I won't do that to you.'

'So, what you're doing now is okay, is it?' His top lip curled and his eyes flashed with sparks of anger. 'Running away again. Leaving because things got a little awkward. That's not how you handle stress that comes into your life, Isla. You have to face it head-on and deal with it.'

Isla raised her chin, determined not to be talked out of going. 'I *am* dealing with it *my* way.'

'Your way?' He gave a scornful laugh. 'Your way is childish and immature. You're having a child yourself. My child. You can't just run away when things don't work out the way you hoped.'

'I'm not running away. I'm removing myself from a situation that will hurt both of us and our child in the long run.' Isla was proud of the evenness of her tone, which belied the storm of emotion building in her chest.

His eyebrows were so tightly knitted there was no space between them. He opened and closed his mouth a couple of times as if searching for the right words. 'You're really serious about this.' It wasn't a question; it sounded more like a statement of resignation. Maybe he knew deep down how hopeless it was. How he might never be able to get rid of those wretched photos.

Isla tried to read his expression, looking for a clue, a hope to hold onto, to convince her he cared enough for her—*loved her enough*—to ride out any scandal, but his features were cast in marble. Impenetrable, unreadable, cold marble. 'I am serious. I'm flying home in a couple of hours. I'll keep you informed on the baby's progress and send you a copy of the next scan.'

'I want to be there when he or she is born.' There was a strange quality to his voice she hadn't heard before but his expression remained masklike.

She nodded and grasped the strap of the bag slung over her shoulder. 'Of course.'

He stepped forward to pick up her bag. 'I'll take you to the airport.'

Isla put a hand on his arm to stop him. 'No. I'd rather you didn't. I'm not a fan of lengthy goodbyes.'

The muscles in his arm bunched under the touch of her hand and he pulled it away as if she had wounded him. 'Yes, well, I should know that by now. I should be feeling grateful I caught you before you left. Or did you leave me a note like last time?'

Isla pressed her lips together, colour warming her cheeks. 'I was going to text you once I was on board.'

'Magnanimous of you.'

Isla let out a heavy breath and closed her eyes in a slow blink. 'Don't do this, Rafe.'

He gave another scornful laugh. 'Don't do what? My fiancée decides she's calling off our relationship within days of our wedding and I'm not supposed to be angry or upset?'

'I never wanted to be your fiancée in the first place,' Isla said, summoning up some anger of her own. It was either anger or reveal her love and that she was *not* going to do. Not to be rejected like every other time she had opened her heart to someone who didn't love her back. 'You were the one who insisted on marriage. You can still be a father without being a husband. And, I can assure you, you'll be a damn better father without me as your wife.'

'Is this your final decision?' The calm chill was back in his voice and his expression was as blank and cold as the marble pillar behind him.

'There's nothing you could say to change my mind, Rafe.'

One dark eyebrow went up in an arc over his eye. 'Nothing?'

Isla held his cynical look. How could she trust it were true if he said those three little words now? 'Nothing I would believe.'

He pushed his hands into his trouser pockets, rocking back on his heels as if he was waiting for a particularly annoying houseguest to get their act together and leave. 'I'll make sure there is plenty of money in your account to help with expenses.'

'You don't have to do—'

'Don't tell me what I have to do, Isla.' The chord of bitterness in his tone stung like a slap. 'I will provide for my own flesh and blood.' He removed his hands from his pockets and picked up her overnight bag. 'You'd better get going. You don't want to miss your flight.'

Isla walked out to the cab with her heart feeling as heavy as a tombstone. It was as if every sadness she had ever experienced, every disappointment, every rejection had gathered in her chest. Weighing her down with the reminder of how dangerous it was to love someone and then lose them.

She got in the cab and Rafe closed the door and stepped back, his hands going back into his trouser pockets, his spy face back on. 'Safe travels.'

Isla forced a polite on-off smile to her lips. 'Thank you.'

He turned and walked back into the villa and shut the door before the cab driver had even put the car in gear.

Rafe held his breath until he heard the cab drive off and then he swore. Loud and filthy and in three languages. There weren't enough words in all the languages in the world for him to express how angry he was feeling. Every muscle in his body was coiling with it, his guts burning and churning. He was angry that Isla had once again caught him off-guard and dropped a bomb on him. The *I'm leaving you* bomb. The bomb that exploded in his chest and made it impossible for him to breathe. An invisible steel band was around his heart, tightening, tightening, tightening until he was starved of oxygen. He had never had a panic attack in his life but this sure felt like it. What was wrong with him? He'd experienced Isla leaving before and got through it. He would get through it again.

He *had* to.

Rafe shoved a hand through his hair so hard he was surprised his fingers didn't come away dripping blood and hair roots. He wanted to punch the wall in frustration but he didn't think his hand would appreciate the contact with solid Italian marble. He pulled in a ragged breath and fought to calm himself. Okay, so the wedding would have to be cancelled. No problem. He had enough staff to take care of that. There were some tasks best left to others and that was one of them. He wanted no reminders of his failure to keep Isla by his side. He had offered her the world and she had rejected him.

Concetta appeared like a ghost, her face equally pale. 'She's gone?'

Rafe planted his hands on his hips and glared at her. 'I suppose you're happy now. You never liked her, did you?'

His housekeeper had the grace to look ashamed. 'It's true at first I didn't, but I came to realise she loves you and that's all that matters.'

Rafe stared at her as if she had suddenly started speaking in tongues. 'What?'

'She loves you, *signor*. You would have to be blind not to see it.'

'You're mistaken,' Rafe said. 'If she loves me then why the hell did she just leave in a cab for the airport? Huh? Tell me that. Why?'

'Did you tell her you love her?'

Rafe let out a frustrated breath. 'What is this female obsession with that word? I'm prepared to marry her, provide for her, and protect her and our baby. Why isn't that enough?'

Concetta folded her arms and shook her head, clearly disappointed in him. 'Loving someone isn't just about words, it's about actions. Your actions speak louder than any words but she still needs to hear you say it.'

His actions? What did his actions say other than he was prepared to take responsibility for the child he had helped conceive? He cared for Isla, wanted her, needed her like he needed his next breath...but love? That was a word he shied away from. It was a word that was used far too freely and easily. He had heard it throughout his childhood from his father, too many times to count. And yet, when forced to make a choice between his two families, his father's 'love' for Rafe had not lasted the distance. It had vaporised like a ghost in a cheap horror movie.

'You've still got time to catch her if you hurry.' Concetta's voice interrupted his thoughts.

Rafe shut the idea down quick-smart. Gone were

the days when he would beg someone to stay with him. 'She's made her choice. For once, I'm going to respect it.'

Isla landed in London and found a cheap hotel to stay in but her heart was still back in Sicily. There was an emptiness in her chest that nothing could fill. Even her baby seemed overly restless, as if wondering where its father had gone. The one good thing about her trip back was there didn't seem to be any sign of her scandal following her. No paparazzi to hound her. No billboards or newsflash sheets outside shops documenting her shame. The newspapers here had other scandals to report but it was of small comfort.

She sat on the bed in her small hotel room and checked her phone. No missed calls and no messages from Rafe. She sighed and tossed the phone to one side and lay down, too weary to take off her travel-worn clothes and get into bed. She was just drifting off to sleep when she heard her phone buzzing and she snatched it up. 'Oh, hi, Layla...'

'Gosh, that was enthusiastic. Has someone died?' Layla said.

'Almost.' Isla sighed. 'And it was my fault.'

'Eek! What happened?'

Isla filled her friend in on Rafe's grandmother's health scare. 'So, you see, I had to leave because it will only happen again. I can't make my past go away.'

'No, but Rafe might be able to,' Layla said. 'It will cost him but if he loves you then what's a few million pounds here or there?'

'He doesn't love me.' Isla gave another sigh. 'He feels responsible for me. He cares about me and the baby, but love… I don't think so. If he did, why didn't he ever tell me?'

'You know what your problem is? I have the same problem so I should know,' Layla said. 'You haven't experienced a loving and secure childhood so you don't recognise love when it's right smack bang in front of you. You don't trust it even when you *can* see it. I reckon a man who spends squillions of pounds to protect you from humiliation is either completely nuts or madly in love.'

Could it be true? Did Rafe love her? 'But he never said he loved me,' Isla said.

'Did you tell him you loved him?'

'No, but—'

'Hah! There's your problem right there.' She imagined Layla snapping her fingers for effect. 'You're both too proud to fess up to how you feel. Someone has to make the first move to be vulnerable.'

'You sound like such an expert on relationships all of a sudden.'

'Och aye, I'm an expert all right.' Layla gave a self-deprecating laugh. 'Not that I've had any romantic relationships or ever likely to.'

Isla ended the call a short time later and got off the

bed with her phone held against her chest. Should she call Rafe? She bit her lip and looked at the phone— she was a call away from adding even more pain to her life. Wasn't it better to leave things as they were? She had said all she needed to say. They would never have resumed their relationship if it hadn't been for the baby. She would just be another ex-lover he forgot about in time.

But she would need all the time in the world to forget about him.

CHAPTER THIRTEEN

RAFE DIDN'T EVEN bother going to bed to try and sleep. For the first three nights he avoided the bedroom he had shared with Isla and sat brooding in an armchair, occasionally drifting off out of sheer exhaustion, only to wake up and find himself back where he'd started three months ago.

But feeling worse.

Much worse.

It was like he had some sort of sickness. His muscles ached, his chest burned, his mouth was dry, his eyes bloodshot and sore. He'd stopped shaving two days ago because he couldn't stand the sight of himself when he looked in the mirror. He looked like a dog that had been kicked to the kerb one too many times.

He sat at his desk and put his head in his hands. As relationship hangovers went, this one was off the scale. Every bone in his skull was tightening against his brain like a clamp on a peach. He literally didn't know how he was going to function without Isla. She added colour to the bland palette of his life. His villa felt like a prison, his housekeeper a mean prison guard who kept shaking her head and tut-tutting not quite under her breath.

Rafe's phone buzzed with an incoming call and he snatched it up off the desk with his heart racing. But his stomach fell in disappointment when he saw his father's number come up on the screen. The last thing he needed right now was a call from his father. He turned the phone to silent and sought a perverse enjoyment watching it ring out. It was payback for all the times he'd wanted to speak to his father but his father had been 'too busy' to speak to him.

Childish of him, perhaps, but like father, like son as the saying went.

He pushed back his chair and walked over to the window, not one bit surprised to see it was raining. The gloomy weather suited his mood. It would be an insult to what he was suffering if the sun came out any time soon.

The phone rang again and he swore and turned around and picked it up. His father again. He sighed and answered. 'Father.' He never called him Dad or Papà. Not since he was thirteen.

'I heard about your broken engagement and I wanted to send my deepest sympathy,' his father said. 'You must be really hurting.'

'Deepest sympathy' was rather apt. It certainly

felt like someone had died. 'Thank you but I'm fine. Not hurting at all.'

His father sighed. 'I know I made you this way and I'm sorry.'

Rafe frowned. 'Made me what way? What are you talking about? Look, I don't have time for this right now so—'

'I deserve that and more from you, Rafe. But please hear me out. I have always regretted needing your stepmother's money more than I needed your mother's love. It ruined everyone's life in the end. Yours, your mother's, your stepmother's and half-brothers'. And mine. I don't want you to end up like me. Surrounded by money and possessions but with no one who truly loves you. They only love the life-style I provide. Your mother loved me for me, with all my faults. It was a gift I threw away and I've regretted it ever since.'

'You've left it a bit late to air your regrets. Mamma has been dead for twenty years.' Rafe didn't strip back the bitterness in his tone; instead he laid it on thick.

'I know and that is an even bigger regret.' His father gave a ragged sigh. 'I thought I was making the right decision at the time. I could only provide for you and your mother and my other family if I stayed in the marriage. If I got a divorce it would have ruined us all. You wouldn't have had that private education in England for one. I would have had to sell your mother's apartment. Your half-brothers wouldn't have been able to achieve the things they've done without my financial backing. I weighed up the options and did what I thought was best under the circumstances. I never stopped loving you, Rafe. I felt ashamed of what I'd done to you and to your mother and it made me avoid you because I was too cowardly to face you. To see the derision and disgust you felt for me.'

Rafe leaned back in his chair and stretched his legs out like a bored teenager. 'It's a good speech since you've had twenty years to prepare it.' He knew he was being ungracious but the hurt was so much a part of him now he didn't know who he was without it.

'Don't make the same mistake by being too proud to accept when you've got it wrong,' his father said. 'Fight for love. Put everything on the line for it. Don't let it slip out of your hands because of stubborn pride.'

Rafe kicked a stack of paperwork beside his desk with his foot, watching it tumble to the floor. 'Look, I appreciate you taking the time to call but—'

'But you don't love her? Is that what you're saying?'

Rafe rubbed at the back of his neck where his muscles were clenched like a boxing champion's fists. What did he feel for Isla other than an ache deep in his chest because she wasn't here? An emptiness inside that prevented him from walking into the bedroom, where he could still smell her perfume. Where he could still see her jewellery and clothes in the wardrobe next to his. He would either have to move house or face up to what he was feeling. What he had been doing his best to ignore from the moment he'd met her.

He loved her.

He loved her so much it had terrified him into denying it. She had challenged him from day one to move out of emotional lockdown into emotional freedom but he had fought it every step of the way. But he could no longer hide his feelings. He had to tell her and hope she felt the same way about him. If she didn't, then he would have to deal with it, allow her the freedom to be the mother of his child without the pressure of being his wife. But he longed for her to be his wife. He longed for her to be by his side for the rest of his life.

'I do love her, Papà,' Rafe said. How strange that the first person he told was the last person he'd thought he would ever want to tell. 'I love her and I have to go and find her before it's too late. I'll call you, okay? Maybe we could meet up some time?'

'I would like that, Rafe.' There was a catch in his father's voice. 'I would like that very much.'

Isla was packed and ready to catch the train to Edinburgh once she checked out of her hotel. She was tired of the bustling energy of London when all she wanted to do was hide under a duvet and cry. There were too many reminders of happy couples walking hand in hand down the street or sitting in crowded cafés holding hands across the table. Even the weather she took as a personal insult. How dare the sun shine when she was feeling so wretched and lonely? It might as well be grey and dismal and rainy for the rest of her life.

Isla sighed and went to pick up her bag to make her way to the train station, but just then there was a knock on the door. She only had one overnight bag and her tote so hadn't called for a porter. She stepped past her bag on the floor and opened the door and her heart leapt into her throat. 'Rafe?'

'May I come in?'

She stepped aside and waved him in, not sure what to make of his expression. He looked like he hadn't slept since she left. The area underneath his eyes was as dark as a bruise and there were lines bracketing his mouth as if he had lost weight. She closed the door and faced him. 'How did you find me?'

He glanced at the bag on the floor. 'You're leaving?' His voice sounded hollow and his throat moved up and down as if something was caught in his gullet.

'I'm going back to Edinburgh on the overnight train.'

'Isla, don't go back to Scotland. Come home

with me. Please. I shouldn't have let you leave without—'

'Rafe, we've already had this conversation,' Isla said, turning away with a sigh. 'I've made up my mind and you have to accept it. I'm not the right wife for you. I will only bring misery and suffering into your life.'

'I'm miserable and suffering without you,' Rafe said. 'I haven't slept. I haven't eaten. I miss you so much. I love you. I've been hiding from it all this time. I fell in love with you the moment I met you and I've been resisting acknowledging it ever since. Can you ever forgive me?'

Isla slowly turned back to face him. 'You love me? Are you sure you're not just saying that to get your way?'

He gave a humourless laugh. 'I guess I deserve that. The first time I've ever told a woman I love her and she thinks I don't mean it. I love you and I want to spend the rest of my life proving it to you. I can't bear the thought of spending another day without you. You're everything to me. I'm only half a person without you.'

Isla tried to control the tremble of her bottom lip but couldn't quite manage it. Tears sprang from her eyes and she brushed at them with the back of her hand. 'Why have you waited until now to tell me? Why didn't you tell me four days ago?'

'Has it only been four days?' He took her by the

hands and drew her closer. 'It felt like four decades. I was a fool back then and an even bigger fool three months ago by not finding you when you left and telling you how I feel.' He held her gaze with his own shining with tenderness. 'When we first met you rocked me out of my emotional deep freeze. I fought it, denied it for as long as I could. Loving someone terrified me because it gave them the power to hurt me if they left. I felt that when my father left all those years ago and I made a promise to myself to never experience that pain again. And yet, I ended up losing you—the love of my life.'

Isla wound her arms around his neck and pressed close to his body. 'You haven't lost me, darling. I'm right here. I love you too. Like you, I've been hiding from it, too frightened to be rejected like all those times when I was a kid.'

He kissed her soundly, his arms wrapped around her as if he never wanted to let her go. After a long moment, he drew back to look down at her. 'I have something to tell you. That lowlife creep will never harass you again. There are a number of charges against him on other matters that will put him away for a long time. I can't guarantee the photos won't surface some other time but this time we will face it together. We will ride it out because we are a team that can't be disbanded. No scandal or misstep in the past will be big enough to tear us apart.'

Could it be true? She would never have to face the

shame of her past alone? Isla suddenly felt stronger than she had ever felt. She knew she could face anything with Rafe by her side. 'Oh, Rafe, I don't know how to thank you.'

He cradled her face in his hands, looking deeply into her eyes, his own eyes glistening with moisture. 'When you left the second time, I didn't realise the significance of what you said until later. You said, *"You'll be a damn better father without me as your wife,"* and it made me realise how much you tried to protect me from your past. That you acted in what you thought were my best interests. I'm sorry I didn't see that at the time. My father said something similar to me yesterday about why he did what he did and I realised I've been a bit blind and stubborn about him too. I allowed my anger to overshadow everything else. Can you ever forgive me for letting you go, not once, but twice?'

'Of course, I forgive you.' Isla pressed a series of kisses to his lips. 'I love you.'

'I love you too, you probably have no idea how much.' He gave another wry laugh. 'I'm only starting to realise it myself. I can't believe I was so blind to my own feelings. It's like I was a robot walking through life before I met you. I didn't feel much for anyone. I didn't allow myself to get close to people. But a few minutes in your company and all that changed. And it freaked me out so much I denied it.' Rafe hugged her close to his chest. 'My stubbornness nearly ruined both our lives. I will do everything I can to make it up to you. You'll just need to give me the next fifty or so years to do it, okay?'

Isla looked up at him with a smile so wide she thought her face would crack. 'You're on.'

* * * * *

If you enjoyed
Cinderella's Scandalous Secret
by Melanie Milburne
you're sure to enjoy these other
Secret Heirs of Billionaires stories!

Shock Heir for the King
by Clare Connelly
Demanding His Hidden Heir
by Jackie Ashenden
The Maid's Spanish Secret
by Dani Collins
Sheikh's Royal Baby Revelation
by Annie West

Available now!

COMING NEXT MONTH FROM

⊞ HARLEQUIN

Presents®

Available October 22, 2019

#3761 CHRISTMAS BABY FOR THE GREEK
by Jennie Lucas

A year after his incredible encounter with Holly, billionaire Stavros discovers she's had his child! But he'll have to break down the emotional walls he's spent years building if he's to claim his bride and son...

#3762 HIS CONTRACT CHRISTMAS BRIDE
Conveniently Wed!
by Sharon Kendrick

As new guardian to his orphaned nephew, CEO Drakon must marry! And sweet Lucy is the ideal candidate. But Lucy soon realizes she can't be just a wife in name only. Can guarded Drakon give anything more to his contract bride?

#3763 BOUND BY THEIR NINE-MONTH SCANDAL
One Night with Consequences
by Dani Collins

Heiress Pia is duty-bound to marry well. And illegitimate Angelo is completely unsuitable husband material. Yet this Spaniard's seduction leaves her pregnant! Now to control the headlines, Pia must step into the spotlight—with the wedding of the century!

#3764 CONFESSIONS OF A PREGNANT CINDERELLA
Rival Spanish Brothers
by Abby Green

"I'm pregnant. With your child." Waitress Skye has imagined this moment—her chance to finally tell billionaire Lazaro that their night together had consequences. But what Lazaro says to her next is even more shocking...

HPCNMRA1019

#3765 UNWRAPPING THE INNOCENT'S SECRET
Secret Heirs of Billionaires
by Caitlin Crews
It infuriates self-made billionaire Pascal that he can't forget the forbidden passion he once shared with innocent Cecilia. This Christmas, he's determined to shake off those memories... until they shockingly come face-to-face—and Cecilia reveals her six-year secret!

#3766 CLAIMING MY HIDDEN SON
The Notorious Greek Billionaires
by Maya Blake
My marriage to Calypso was simply business—until our unexpectedly passionate wedding night! Unwilling to muddy our convenient arrangement, I left. Now discovering the baby in my estranged wife's arms, I will claim my son—and Calypso, too...

#3767 BRIDE BEHIND THE BILLION-DOLLAR VEIL
Crazy Rich Greek Weddings
by Clare Connelly
To complete his empire, fantastically wealthy Thanos must counter his scandalous reputation—with a wife! His assistant, Alice, is the perfect choice. Until he lifts her veil and their intense, electrifying kiss complicates *everything*...

#3768 THE ITALIAN'S CHRISTMAS PROPOSITION
by Cathy Williams
When Matteo's rescue of Rosie puts his business deal in jeopardy, he sees only one solution—making her his fake fiancée! But will their unexpected connection tempt Matteo to put a ring on Rosie's finger—for real?

Get 4 FREE REWARDS!

We'll send you 2 FREE Books
plus 2 FREE Mystery Gifts.

Heiress Pia is duty bound to marry well—and illegitimate Angelo is completely unsuitable husband material. But this Spaniard's seduction leaves her pregnant...and now, to control the headlines, Pia must step into the spotlight—with the wedding of the century!

Read on for a sneak preview of
Dani Collins's next story for Harlequin Presents
Bound by Their Nine-Month Scandal

"Señor Navarro," she said, offering her hand.

"Angelo," he corrected. His clasp sent electricity through to her nerve endings as he took the liberty of greeting her with "Pia."

"Thank you for coming," she said, desperately pretending they were strangers when all she could think about was how his weight had pressed her into the cushions while her entire being had seemed to fly.

His eyes dazzled yet pinned her in place. There was an air of aggression about him. Hostility even, in the way he had appeared like this, when she had literally been on the defensive. He seemed ready for a fight.

She had almost hoped he would leave her hanging after her note. She could have raised their baby with a clear conscience that she had tried to reach out, while facing no interference from this unknown quantity.

As for what would happen if he did get in touch? She had tried to be realistic in her expectations, but Poppy had stuck a few delusions in her head. They seemed even more ridiculous as she faced such a daunting conversation with him. How had she even found the courage to say such frank things that night, let alone do the things they'd done? Wicked, intimate, carnal things that caused a blush to singe up from her throat into her cheeks.

"I need a moment," she said, voice straining.

She had already declined invitations for drinks, fearful her avoidance of a glass of champagne would make her condition obvious. She only had to say a last goodbye to the committee and

"Thank you again, but I must take this meeting."

Moments later, trembling inwardly, she led Angelo into the small office off the lab where she had worked the past three years when not in the field. She had already packed her things into a small cardboard box, which sat on the chair. She was shifting from academic work to motherhood and marriage. That was all that was left of her former life.

Angelo seemed to eat up all the air as he closed the door behind him and looked at the empty bulletin board, the box of tissues and the well-used filing cabinet.

Pia started to move the box, but he said, "I'll stand."

He was taller than her, which made him well over six feet, because she had the family's genetic disposition toward above-average height. His air of watchfulness was intimidating, too, especially when he trained his laser-blue eyes on her again.

"Your card was very cryptic," he said.

She had spent a long time composing it, wondering why he had sneaked into the ball when he could easily have afforded the plate fee. At the time, she had thought his reason for being on the rooftop was exactly as he had explained it—curiosity. She had many more questions now, but didn't ask them yet. There was every chance she would never see him again after she told him why she had reached out.

Memories of their intimacy that night accosted her daily. It was top of mind now, which put her at a further disadvantage. Her only recourse was to do what she always did when she was uncomfortable—hide behind a curtain of reserve and speak her piece as matter-of-factly as possible.

"I'll come straight to the point." She hitched her hip on the edge of her desk and set her clammy palms together, affecting indifference while fighting to keep a quaver from her voice.

"I'm pregnant. It's yours."

Don't miss
Bound by Their Nine-Month Scandal
available November 2019 wherever
Harlequin Presents® *books and eBooks are sold.*

www.Harlequin.com

HPEXP1019

5947

Want to give in to temptation with
steamy tales of irresistible desire?

Check out **Harlequin® Presents®**,
Harlequin® Desire and
Harlequin® Kimani™ Romance books!

New books available every month!

CONNECT WITH US AT:

Facebook.com/groups/HarlequinConnection

Facebook.com/HarlequinBooks

Twitter.com/HarlequinBooks

Instagram.com/HarlequinBooks

Pinterest.com/HarlequinBooks

ReaderService.com

**ROMANCE WHEN
YOU NEED IT**

PGENRE2018